Bryce seemed to explode at Marie from across [...] room, one moment a rock of impenetrable stillness, the next, a rush of intensely heated ire. His hands gripped her arms until her bones ached. His face pressed near hers, a mask of ugly accusations and disbelief. "You're lying."

Fear writhed in the pit of her stomach. Yet, with vivid clarity, she understood and sympathized with his contradicting emotions. Bryce was afraid to believe. She touched his face with gentle fingertips, instilling a sense of reality to her words. "He's alive, Bryce. Ryan is your son."

Dear Reader,

Welcome to March! Spring is in the air. The birds are chirping, the bees are buzzing . . . and men and women all over the world are thinking about—love.

Here at Silhouette Desire we take love *very* seriously. We're committed to bringing you six terrific stories all about love each and every month of the year, and this March is no exception.

Let's start with March's *Man of the Month* by Jackie Merritt. It's called *Tennessee Waltz,* and I know you're going to love this story. Next, Naomi Horton returns with *Chastity's Pirate.* (How can you resist a book with a title like this? You just *can't!*) And look for books by Anne Marie Winston, Barbara McCauley, Justine Davis and new-to-Desire Kat Adams.

And in months to come, some of your very favorite authors are coming your way. Look for sensuous romances from the talented pens of Dixie Browning, Lass Small, Cait London, Barbara Boswell . . . just to name a few.

So go wild with Desire, and start thinking about love.

All the best,

Lucia Macro
Senior Editor

KAT ADAMS

THURSDAY'S CHILD

SILHOUETTE *Desire*
Published by Silhouette Books New York
America's Publisher of Contemporary Romance

SILHOUETTE BOOKS
300 East 42nd St., New York, N.Y. 10017

THURSDAY'S CHILD

Copyright © 1993 by Kat Adams

ISBN: 0-373-05773-3

First Silhouette Books printing March 1993

All the characters in this book have no existence outside the imagination of the author and have no relation whatsoever to anyone bearing the same name or names. They are not even distantly inspired by any individual known or unknown to the author, and all incidents are pure invention.

® and ™: Trademarks used with authorization. Trademarks indicated with ® are registered in the United States Patent and Trademark Office, the Canada Trade Mark Office and in other countries.

Printed in the U.S.A.

KAT ADAMS

was always an enthusiastic reader of romances. To her, coming home to a good romance was like leaving the Twilight Zone of housekeeping and entering Disneyland. Eventually, she decided that if reading romances was pleasurable, then writing them would be pure delight.

Prologue

Marlena Stynhearst had never thought she'd be comparing herself to something as disgusting as a cornered rat, but that was exactly how she was feeling. She was literally backed against the wall of her own fortress. As her eyes swept the posh furnishings of her Los Angeles office, she found her little kingdom lacked anything that might help her now. Words were her only defense, words and a grit that had sprung up from the terrible sensation of being duped.

"You're insane, Rex," she snapped, fighting to release her hands from his shackling fist.

"You'd like to believe that, wouldn't you, Marlena?" he murmured against the soft flesh beneath her ear. "But it's just greed. You're a product of greed, darling. You understand."

Marlena shivered. A month ago this man's touch would have sent a welcomed, tantalizing chill over her body. Tonight, the chill was there, but it was one of revulsion. With a bravado that sounded ridiculous given her present position, she replied frostily, "No, I don't understand. My brother was supposed to have been your friend, yet I learn that you had coerced him out of enormous control of Stynhearst Industries. Is that what you've planned for me? I'll warn you, you'll not find *me* so easily managed.''

Rex Kane chuckled, ignoring her starchy declaration. ''Andrew was a fool. He allowed his obsession with gambling and his demanding wife to manipulate him.'' His amusement swept into a laugh of demonic gusto. ''You know, I wish old Andrew were still around so I could send him a thank-you note. It was truly considerate of him to get himself and his nuisance of a wife killed in that accident three years ago. The company people had begun to wonder why he didn't show more interest in the business. Now, with Andrew and Eva dead and Stynhearst in your hands, no one thinks it strange that the pretty young heiress has fallen madly in love with her CEO.''

Marlena found a sneer came easily when turned on the despised deeds of an enemy. ''I did fall into your hands like a ripe plum, didn't I?'' she demanded bitterly.

''Oh, darling, don't be so hard on yourself,'' he crooned in feigned commiseration. ''After Andrew's death, you were so wrapped up in taking care of your orphaned nephew and finishing your last two years of college that you allowed me to take over even more control of Stynhearst. You did the logical thing. The thing I was counting on you to do.''

''And wasn't it so generous of you to offer to personally show me the ropes of Stynhearst after I graduated, all the while pretending to fall in love with me?'' Marlena added, aggrieved by her own gullibility.

''It's my irresistible charm, darling,'' Rex murmured. He, used his free hand to whisk aside her long brunette curls so he could roam the territory of her exposed throat. ''Remember to be more careful the next time a man uses it on you.''

''You can be certain I will.'' She turned away from his descending mouth, not attempting to hide her repugnance to his touch. ''I promise I'll not soon forget any of your lessons, Rex,'' she whispered.

He drew back, tightening the hold on her wrists until she thought they would snap. ''You're not a fool, Marlena, so remember this lesson,'' he growled, laying his free hand upon her breast. ''If you don't give me everything my little heart desires, I'll see to it that you lose your little heart's desire."

Ryan. He was speaking of her nephew, Ryan. Marlena's heart beat in frantic dread, but still she couldn't back down. "Your smugness is premature, Rex. Don't forget I found the tape of you telling Andrew that the child he thought he'd adopted had actually been stolen from a couple in Connecticut." She looked at her former friend and fiancé, unable to believe the depths of his duplicity. "Every time you wanted something, you used that tape to threaten Andrew with losing Ryan."

Rex rolled his eyes upward and sighed in dramatic bliss. "Isn't love marvelous, darling? When used properly, it can lay the world at one's feet. All it takes is a victim who's willing to sacrifice everything in the name of love. In this case, it was our own dear Andy who sacrificed Stynhearst for the love of his gambling, his wife's money to pay his debts and his best friend—me—who provided the child, which kept Eva happy."

He ran his knuckles along the ridge of her cheek. "If you'd not been so nosy, darling, you'd never have known you were sacrificing Stynhearst for Ryan. But you had to snoop around in my safe. Looking for the boy's birth certificate?" he guessed.

When she nodded hesitantly, he continued. "I'd gotten Ryan into that fancy school for gifted children last year without one, didn't I? What made you think I couldn't do so again?"

Marlena jerked away from his hand. It amazed her how he could flit through trifling details while disregarding the magnitude of his atrocious actions. "What kind of monster are you?" she hissed. "You kidnapped a baby to use in trapping my brother, then you secretly taped that conversation between yourself and Andrew where you confessed to taking Ryan. With the tape, you had proof that Andrew was aware of Ryan's true parentage, and by Andrew's silence, he as good as sanctioned your crime."

"Very good, Marlena. I knew you were a smart girl. So, you must also understand that now that you've listened to

the tape and know the truth about Ryan, you've replaced
Andrew in that same incriminating boat.''

Green eyes as hard and glittery as emeralds bore into Rex
Kane with little effect. Yes, I have replaced my brother in
that boat, haven't I? she impotently seethed in silence. After listening to the tape, she'd had no doubts as to why Rex
had held on to the damning evidence. Tonight her theory
had proven correct. Rex was using it to give her an ultima-
tum: marry him, allow him complete control of Stynhearst, or lose Ryan.

She hiked her chin up a notch. ''Your blackmail is dou-
ble-edged, though, Rex. You can't take Ryan away from me,
because if you do, I'll use the tape to implicate you in his
kidnapping.''

He shrugged. ''Andrew tried that approach with me. I'll
tell you what I told him. I've spent the last four years using
that little boy to gain control of Stynhearst. You can turn the
tape over to the police, and I'll end up losing everything and
spending time in jail.'' He used his tall, muscular body to
crowd her closer into the corner, then whispered, ''But the
authorities would be duty-bound to return little Ryan to his
grief-stricken parents, wouldn't they, darling? Can you give
up Ryan?''

A futile hate left Marlena standing in muted helplessness.

''I don't think you can, Marlena,'' he continued specu-
latively. ''You're so transparent, so easily read. I knew by
that strange mood swing you experienced a week ago that
something was wrong. When I discovered the tape and
newspaper article of the kidnapping missing from my safe,
I had my answer. For a week I watched you struggle with
indecision. For a whole week you've known the truth,
but—'' he tipped up her chin until she was forced to meet his
eyes ''—you haven't told anyone, have you? If you haven't
found the nerve to turn the evidence over to the police yet,
then I don't think you will.''

No, she hadn't found the nerve. Ryan's natural parents
had known him eighteen months before they'd lost him.
Andrew and Eva had claimed an equal amount of time in
Ryan's life. But Marlena had held that child in her arms for

three wonderful years. Though no biological ties existed between them, she and Ryan shared a kinship that ran deeper than the bonds of blood. Marlena had at last found a family in Ryan, and to Ryan, she was his rock in a world of shifting sand. They needed each other; it was as simple as that.

Now her life was being swept up in a fiendish eddy of fear created by one man's evilness. She was being forced to fight a battle against him that she could not win, but would not surrender. "I won't marry you, Rex," she responded defiantly. "Even if I don't turn you in, I'll still not marry you and give you this company."

An unnerving smile settled on Rex's lips. His fingers found the pulse points of her throat and applied enough pressure to communicate a warning. "I admire your bravery, but you are so very naive. You see, darling, like Andrew, I enjoy gambling, but I play for even higher stakes. In this game I'm playing with you, I'm betting on an all-or-nothing proposition. I'll either forfeit my position and my freedom, or I'll gain the whole company and its beautiful heiress as my bride."

He chuckled as he turned his threatening grasp into a parody of a caress. "I can see by the look on your face that you're beginning to understand me. That's good. A wife should understand her husband."

He abruptly shifted his arm, snaring Marlena's waist. He made sure that this time, his kiss wouldn't be denied. He ground his lips against hers, hurting her, subduing her with his superior strength. She struggled, but he followed her movement with painful persistence, allowing her no relief from the suffocating pressure of his body.

Just when Marlena thought she'd faint from the lack of breath, he loosened his hold but kept her within the circle of his arm. He taunted her with his supremacy. "Tomorrow, you will return the tape and the news article to me. In a few weeks, we'll marry as planned. After our honeymoon, you will begin the process of turning over full reign of Stynhearst Industries to me. Then you can continue being a little mother to the boy. You will be managed, Marlena, *or you will lose Ryan.*"

His finger traced the length of the gold chain around her neck, following its links to where they disappeared between her breasts as he leisurely added, "I might point out that there are several ways to lose a child. I never got around to producing any legal documents, such as Ryan's adoption papers and birth certificate. Without them, Andrew couldn't even claim the boy as his son. So, as far as the world is concerned, Ryan ceased to exist several years ago. I can easily make that a fact, Marlena."

His hand moved behind his back, then suddenly reappeared, holding a knife before her eyes. Marlena stiffened as the shiny blade winked at her with macabre seductiveness before vanishing from her sight. "Just so you won't misjudge the limits of my ambition, darling."

The knife pressed against the side of Marlena's hip, hissing as it severed the fabric of her skirt and almost delicately nipped into the flesh beneath. A small whimper escaped her throat, more from fright than pain, as the wound awakened her to the reality of how far this man would go to force her into submission.

"I'll enjoy admiring that little scar on our honeymoon, Marlena," he purred, then released her and started for the door. "I'm glad I decided to initiate this little discussion tonight. You'd stewed long enough, and I wanted to relieve your mind by letting you know that everything is settled."

He swung around once more to face her. "Oh. One more lesson before I leave, darling," he said. "You allowed yourself to become too attached to Ryan and it cost you. Never care for someone to the point that they become indispensable."

The door closed, leaving Marlena in the stark loneliness of dealing with her plight. She touched her hip, then examined the blood on her fingertips dispassionately. Rex Kane had made two mistakes this evening. One, he naturally assumed that all people's selfishness and greed, whatever form they took, rivaled his own. And two, he had threatened Ryan's life.

The combination of these two errors would cause Rex Kane's downfall—Marlena would see to it. For although Rex was right, she did love Ryan desperately and did find him indispensable to her existence, she would not allow Rex to use Ryan as a pawn.

To protect Ryan, Marlena would have to give him up.

She had known for days that this was inevitable. Ryan's parents deserved their child back after four and a half anguish-filled years. Rex Kane deserved to forfeit ten times as many years of his freedom in payment for that anguish.

She picked up the phone, intending to seek the advice of her attorney, but dropped it back into its cradle before she completed the call. Rex's words rang like a death knell inside her head: the moment the authorities learn Ryan's identity, they would whisk him away to his parents.

Marlie ran her fingers through her tangled hair in agitation. She needed time. Time to make certain Ryan was going to a good home. Time to meet Ryan's parents, to get to know them and they to know her, before she reintroduced them to their son.

Then, if she had properly paved the way for understanding, maybe Bryce and Janette Powell would find room in Ryan's new life for an illegitimate Aunt Marlie.

One

Honk! Honk! Honk!

Marlena Theodora Stynhearst—or just plain Marlie now, since her recent topple from society—gave the irate motorist behind her an equally irate scowl via the sideview mirror of her stalled pickup truck. Having done her dirtiest retaliation for the moment, she continued fanning herself with a Connecticut road map and contemplating why it was in such bad taste to feel sorry for oneself. Personally, she thought she'd more than earned the right.

Slap . . . slap . . . slap.

"That guy behind us is extremely rude, isn't he, Aunt Marlie?"

Marlie smiled feebly across the worn truck seat at her young nephew who was contenting himself with slapping a baseball into his mitted hand. She knew better than to totally concur with Ryan Bartholomew Stynhearst's assessment of the honker's manners. Ryan could appear as angelic as one of Gabriel's own, with a little ball cap squashing his adorable curls into a golden halo around his head. Marlie knew better, though. This intellectually brilliant six-year-old knew such diabolical means of seeking restitution that it made her skin crawl. She tempered her agreement with an attempt at charity that she hoped the honker behind her appreciated.

"It's terribly hot, Ryan," she explained patiently. "Heat has a way of bringing out the beast in all of us." She could tell this recital of adult logic had no appreciable effect on the child. Ryan, as with most children, had a natural immunity to environmental conditions that drove grown-ups crazy. She tried another approach. "He's probably in a hurry to get home to his wonderful swimming pool and a cold can of root beer."

Ryan pursed his lips, squinted his big blue eyes and furrowed his brow, a prelude to the dreaded *w* word. "Why doesn't he just back up and go another way, then?" he demanded, clearly put out with anyone who couldn't figure out a simple solution to the problem.

Marlie was left with her usual, inadequate response. "I don't know."

She also didn't know why she had to come up with the bright idea of talking that sweet old man, who was selling produce on the corner across from the Sunnydale bus station, into letting her rent his truck for a few hours, either. She could have carried the six suitcases of paraphernalia she and Ryan had accumulated on their trip easier than fighting this mean-natured truck.

Five minutes had passed since the truck conked out in the middle of the alley, leaving them sweltering in the early-July heat. A helpful young man at a gas station had suggested this alley as a shortcut to the only motel across town. Of course, he'd neglected to mention the potholes as big as moon craters dotting the alley. The last pothole she'd hit must have shaken loose something important in the truck, for it had figuratively put its foot down and refused to budge.

Slap...slap...slap.
Honk! Honk! Honk!

Marlie squeezed her eyes shut and continued fanning herself with one hand while massaging her throbbing temple with the other. What am I doing here? she silently moaned. But she knew all too well what she was doing here.

From California to Connecticut, Marlie's trail had been one of silent tears and constant reminders of what lay at the end—she was going to lose Ryan. This knowledge worried her consciousness like a diagnosed cancer. And anticipating its consequences to her life evoked a fear that closely resembled hopelessness. She was going to lose Ryan, and the best of herself would be lost with him.

She watched Ryan fidget with childish energy and marveled at how she could have been so blessed with his appearance in her life. Ryan needed her, and through him, she vicariously relived the first fourteen years of her contented childhood with Nanny Jane.

Marlie smiled, thinking of darling Jane Pritchett. Jane had been another one of those blessings that Marlie didn't take for granted. The kindly old lady had raised Marlie from infancy when her parents had refused to be fettered by their inconvenient offspring. Thanks to Nanny Jane, Marlie had lived a delightful childhood, full of fun and excitement and learning. Nanny Jane used every opportunity possible to throw open the doors of Marlie's dreary mansion, introducing her charge to fascinating people and experiences.

And along the way Nanny Jane shared her wisdom, teaching Marlie the joys of generosity, the character of compassion and the fulfillment of love. For fourteen years, she was Marlie's family, the two existing in an ordinary world that insulated the child against the more cruel elements of life.

The day Marlie had stood beside her parents flower-decked caskets, she had said a final farewell to those two strangers. And then she said a final farewell to her beloved Nanny Jane.

Andrew, a brother ten years Marlie's senior, couldn't be bothered with a sister he scarcely knew. Nanny Jane was getting old and past her usefulness, Andrew had said. Much better that a budding adolescent of society's elite be tutored in the finer schools of Europe. Without remorse he dismissed the old nanny and sentenced Marlie to four lonely, fearful, disillusioning years at a small, exclusive boarding school in France.

Marlie knew there were many nice, rich people; her new schoolmates were not. Tossed among children whose values and principles were not her own, Marlie soon learned that she must swim with conformity or sink into isolation.

Mostly, Marlie sank.

She couldn't get the hang of judging people according to their position on the social register. She couldn't find the expected satisfaction from vicious gossip or petty revenge. She tried feasting on her worldly possessions and found herself starving for spiritual substance. To her female peers, Marlie was strange—a square peg trying to fit into a round hole. Of course her male peers didn't care if she was strange; she was attractive and rich . . . and fair game.

In the classroom, Marlie drew upon the strength instilled by Nanny Jane and showed the world a smiling face that hid her inner fears. In the dormitory, she learned to live behind a closed door, with loneliness as her closest companion. But always present were the toughness and pride that sustained her ideals and convictions. Marlie survived those four years, but she would never forget them.

Boarding school ended and still she couldn't go home. Go home to what? A brother she didn't know and who didn't want to know her? To a life-style that didn't fit? So she entered a small British university, and studying became her passionate escape from the loneliness of rejection.

The news of Andrew and his wife's accident saddened Marlie, yet with their deaths new life blossomed in her heart. She went home. Home to the wonderful discovery that she was an aunt. Three-year-old Ryan scampered into her life, wearing Spiderman training pants and a dimpled smile that put the silver lining back into Marlie's clouds.

Ryan chased away her bitter, frightening memories of being different from the crowd. Gone were the feelings of uselessness and rejection, the loneliness and fear of being uprooted like a hothouse flower and transplanted on cold, foreign soil. Ryan loved her and needed her, and Marlie soon got back into the business of living life with a purpose again. Recreating the familiar environment of her childhood, Marlie passed on to Ryan Nanny Jane's beautiful legacy of love and devotion, and together aunt and nephew flourished.

Now the hopes of the future were blighted by uncertainties. Marlie twisted the road map in her damp hands, wondering about the Powells. Could they be tolerant, forgiving or accommodating enough to share what Marlie needed most? She needed the child who loved her without reservation, who needed her and allowed her to love him—the child who kept the ghost of her fear of aloneness at bay.

These things she needed, but not more than the greater need to protect the provider. Therefore, she was going to lose Ryan.

The stifling heat of the unair-conditioned truck had kissed the child's freckled nose with beads of sweat. Marlie drank in the sight of the brace of dimples that dented his cheeks as he concentrated on the precision timing of the ball hitting his mitt. Emotion swelled in her throat until she thought it would strangle her. Dear Lord, she loved this child. What would she do when he was gone? *You can't do this,* her brittle bravery fretted. But she would.

"What's wrong, Aunt Marlie?" the boy asked with concern. "Is that guy behind us getting on your nerves?" *Slap . . . slap . . . slap.*

Admonishing herself to snap out of this useless melancholy, she reverted to a more typical behavior. "Ryan," she said in controlled exasperation. "You only know the half of it. I can't start this stupid truck. I can't stop the honker behind me. But I can stop the monotonous racket inside this cab." She plucked the mitt from his hand and slapped it on the seat between them.

The slapping stopped. The honking didn't.

"Want me to have a look under the hood?" Ryan asked, now amusing himself with repeatedly pitching the ball into the air. "It's probably either Carl Carburetor or Bobby Battery."

Marlie stared at him blankly. He informed her, "I know engine parts don't really have proper names, but it helps to remember them."

Right, she thought wryly.

Honk! Honk! Honk!

"I'm going to have to find a mechanic," she muttered wearily.

"What are you going to do about the rude guy behind us?" Ryan asked, thumbing in that direction.

"Do you happen to have a hand grenade in there?" she asked, nudging his duffel bag, which she assumed was filled with boy-type essentials.

Ryan gave her a perplexed look, for though he was a bright lad, it was his aunt who held the honors in subtle sarcasm. "Never mind," she said, grinning and waving away her inquiry. "I'll just have to take the wind out of our honker's sails another way."

Ryan's blue eyes lit up with interest. "Can I help?"

Not knowing how friendly the confrontation between the ill-tempered honker and the damsel in distress would be, Marlie shook her head. "I can handle him alone. Thanks."

Ryan looked disappointed. Marlie smiled as she released the door latch and leapt lightly to the rough surface of the alley. She took a moment to smooth back loose brunette strands into her drooping ponytail while reconnoitering the alley. Marlie had viewed three thousand miles of American scenery after it had already passed her by, for she had spent the four-week trip looking over her shoulder. Rex Kane was out there. Sooner or later he would find her, and she would prefer to meet him face-to-face, rather than have him sneak up from behind.

But Rex Kane wasn't her problem in this alley; the person cursing her in car-horn language was. She set a militant pace to the maroon Saab parked almost on the bumper of her truck.

Honk! Honk—

The last honk of the standard three was cut off as if Marlie's sudden appearance had robbed it of its audacity. Using a neatly manicured fingernail, she tapped on the tinted glass separating her from the driver. The window immediately descended with a soft burr of motion. She pasted on a conservative smile and stooped to look her tormentor in the eye. In this case it turned out to be aviator sunglasses, so she focused intently on her own reflection in them and said sweetly, "Since this arrangement is getting us nowhere, I have a suggestion. Why don't you start my truck for me, and I'll blow your horn for you?"

The sunglasses tilted as the male wearing them considered her from a new angle. A tentative smile appeared, then grew a tad bolder, poking dimples into his bristly cheeks. Always a sucker for a pair of dimples, Marlie took a closer look at her honker. What she saw tempted a grin of her own. Honker was good-looking. Very good-looking in a sweaty ball cap, five o'clock shadow sort of way.

Back off, Stynhearst, she warned herself. A woman with the instincts of a kamikaze pilot when it came to judging the opposite sex had no business giving a male the once-over.

Still, Marlie couldn't help but be intrigued by the man. His smile was wary, with a dash of vulnerability that knocked on the door of her heart. She could relate to wariness and vulnerability. But with enough troubles on her mind she turned a deaf ear to the echoes in her heart and firmly suppressed the urge to return his smile. Instead she raised an eyebrow, challenging him to either admit he was a cad or do something about it.

"I made a mistake," he said by way of meager apology.

Marlie nodded. "Yes, you have, if you think blowing your car horn will intimidate my truck into starting." She turned on the voltage of a deceptively charming smile. "You can see for yourself that it doesn't work."

The lips of the handsome honker twitched again. "That wasn't the mistake I made," he said evenly. "My mistake was thinking you were another one of those annoying people who have the idea that this alley is a parking lot. I've had to turn around three times this week. But today I was hot, tired and feeling just mean enough not to take the long way home."

He paused, gauging her degree of sympathy. Marlie raised a hand to delicately pat away a bored yawn, though her green eyes twinkled with laconic humor at the cad's expense.

He launched a counterattack by pulling off his sunglasses and turned on her two blue eyes that could talk a woman into anything." We also just lost our ball game by one lousy run," he added morosely.

If Marlie had still been a pushover, she may have bought that line and taken the owner of the blue eyes as a bonus. Thanks to her recent education in men, their lines and their looks, she more prudently evaluated what was being offered. She decided she didn't think much of it. "Life can sure be the devil sometimes, can't it?" she responded, pitilessly laughing at his sad tale.

"It's refreshing to find a female who appreciates the delicacy of the male ego," he said dryly. "I have a few tools in my trunk. How about if I give my horn a rest while I take a look at your truck?"

Before she could agree or disagree, he swung open his door, forcing her to step back. Her false smile fell from her face, and she retreated another step as the man straightened to his full height. Rex Kane was six feet tall, but this man would top him by three easy inches. Rex Kane was well built, but this man had more muscles than he could possibly know what to do with. She touched the scar on the side of her hip, vividly recalling the advantages of a man's superior strength. For one heartbeat of time, she intensely resented this man for inspiring the recollection of her helplessness.

Then, just as quickly, the debilitating sensation passed. Slinking off like a simp every time she met someone taller than herself would be admitting that Rex still controlled her life. She absolutely refused to allow it. Nothing was going to mar her remaining time with Ryan. To prove her mettle she turned her attention back to this unnecessarily large male who was standing in the same pothole with her.

His long legs were encased in a pair of those stretchy stirrup pants that ball players wear, his tapered torso plastered with a green jersey. A fashionable length of glossy dark hair fringed a green ball cap, and from the amount of dirt and sweat accentuating all that evident virility, Marlie surmised that he wasn't kidding about the ball game. "You do play ball," she stated unnecessarily, wanting to hear again the pleasant resonance of his Yankee accent.

"Yep," he said over his shoulder as he walked to the rear of his car, unlocked the trunk and retrieved the tools. "And I really am a sore loser, too."

As he passed her on his way to her truck, she tried to check her recoiling steps, but couldn't. She consoled herself by suggesting that there was nothing cowardly about keeping a sensible distance from anything that big and obviously badtempered. Like a little caboose, she trailed behind the man, inquiring politely, "So you were taking your defeat and resulting nastiness out on me and my poor little truck?"

"That's about the size of it," he said with a gruff economy of words.

They reached the truck before Marlie had time to stick out her tongue at the boorish man's back. He handed her the tools, propped his sunglasses on the bill of his cap, then swung open the heavy truck hood with little effort. The damp ball uniform clung to the contours of his muscular body, providing the means for an exhibition in kinetic poetry, while proving his ability to use the power at his disposal. Marlie watched him, experiencing the fear and fascination of a foolish mortal tempted to stroke the beautiful, wild beast.

She swallowed heavily, told herself not to be silly and climbed upon the bumper opposite of where he tinkered with the mystical conglomeration of metal gadgetry. Focusing intently on his busy hands, she asked absently, "Do you think it's Carl Carburetor or Bobby Battery causing the problem?"

The man slowly raised his head to stare at her, and she was subjected to another whammy from those piercing blue eyes. Then his chest began to heave, building pressure for an awesome explosion. It happened, in fact. Reluctant laughter came barreling out, robbing the man of his strength until he had to grasp the truck frame to retain his balance.

Marlie crossed her arms over her chest and patiently waited until the storm of his hilarity calmed. She raised a convincingly disdainful eyebrow. "I know engine parts don't really have proper names, but it helps to remember them." She haughtily quoted Ryan's wisdom.

His smile came easier and more sincerely, as if now that he had finally tried one on for size he found it comfortable. How strange, she thought. She had forty-two sweet little inches worth of reason to smile waiting for her in the truck; even Rex Kane's despicable greed couldn't take that from her. What reason could this obviously healthy, obviously wealthy man have for being so stingy with his humor?

"Sorry if I hurt your feelings," he said, his lips still twitching. "It was just the idea of a little commune residing under the hood of a vehicle that set me off." He leaned over the engine again and added whimsically, "I'd say Connie Coil Wire is our culprit here. You must have disconnected her from Dennis Distributor when you hit the last pothole."

The dimples disappeared again and Marlie thought that rather a shame. To coax them back she tried, "Sounds as if Connie and Dennis were engaged in immoral behavior, anyway. What happens when they disconnect?"

It worked; he repeated that brilliant white smile and augmented it with a wink. "Nothing. Unless Connie is attached... intimately to Dennis, the sparks won't fly. No sparks, no action."

The hesitant smiler had just graduated to a prospective flirt. Marlie decided to quit while she was ahead. She forced her eyes to break their own intimate connection with his. "I believe a union of such significance calls for the assistance of a professional. If you can point me in the direction of a good mechanic, I'll thank you and let you be on your way."

"No need for that." He reached into the truck innards, fiddled a few moments with—Connie and Dennis?—then straightened with a satisfied grunt. "Reunited at last," he said. "You'll start now."

Marlie was impressed. "Thank you," she said, grinning.

She stepped off the bumper and wiped the dust from her hands onto the seat of her cutoff jeans. She had expected the man to rush off to wherever, but he leaned a hand on the truck, crossing his ankles in a relaxed stance that bespoke of nothing but time on his hands. "I couldn't help noticing that this old truck looks exactly like Happy Hanson's," he commented leisurely.

Marlie nodded. "Happy Hanson being the man who sells produce on one of the decently paved streets in this town and who rented me this ornery contraption to move my luggage from the bus station to the motel."

His grimness was back. "You're just passing through Sunnydale?"

She shrugged. "Not exactly. I'll be staying for a few weeks, but the motel will be my address until I find an apartment."

His blue eyes took a visual tour down the length of Marlie's body en route to the toes of his cleated shoes, which he regarded for several moments. Finally he looked at her and remarked, "There's only one apartment complex in Sunnydale."

Marlie was starting to get the message of why he was hanging around and refused to encourage him. "There seems to be only one of everything in Sunnydale," she replied flatly.

"There's only one vacant town house in that one apartment complex," he persisted.

"I'd better hurry then," she countered meaningfully.

Now that he'd gotten the hang of smiling, he didn't seem to want to turn it off. "You're within about twenty potholes of your destination. The rear of the apartments run parallel with this alley. I'll follow you over and tell Mrs. Cobb that I recommend you as a tenant."

"You don't even know me," Marlie protested, surprised.

"I like what I've seen so far." To prove it, he took another thorough look.

With renditions of Rex's deceitfulness performing inside her head, Marlie barely kept the sneer from her voice. "I'm gratified that I meet with your approval. As for taking you up on your suggested lodging tonight, I'll have to ask Ryan. He was looking forward to one last night in a motel bed."

The smile dropped from the man's face as if it had been scraped off with a sharp garden tool. "You're not alone?"

"No, I'm . . ." Marlie's words drifted off as she glanced over the man's shoulder. Just as she was feeling relieved that her deception was going to work, Ryan had to show up and spoil everything. To make matters worse, he was acting his juvenile self. She winced at his appearance. "...with him," she finished lamely, motioning to the boy.

Ryan, how could you? she silently groaned. The child was decked out in a costume she witnessed in only one situation—when he felt threatened by male competition. Ryan's odd apparel consisted of an old Halloween Dracula cape, a black football helmet and a pair of sunglasses. He called this getup his Barf Dater Eliminator uniform, which not only explained Ryan's purpose, but gave fair warning to any offenders.

Oh well, she thought, stifling a wayward bubble of laughter. Maybe this would solve her problem.

It did. Better than she could have imagined.

When she looked back at the man, she had expected at least a wry smile, but she didn't get one. His earlier grim countenance had been mere practice for this one as he stared at Ryan endlessly. Finally, apparently unable to stand the sight of the child a moment longer, he closed the hood of the truck with unwarranted force, turned on his cleated heel and strode toward his car.

Well, this certainly was a new reaction to Ryan's antics. As needful as it had been to end their fruitless tête-à-tête, Marlie hadn't meant to frighten the man, for he had been helpful. "Hey," she called in a jovial voice, "the kid's not really dangerous." No response. "Can I at least ask the name of the man I should thank?" she yelled more loudly.

The man faced her as he flung open his car door. "Powell. Bryce Powell," he answered curtly. "But you can save your thanks." He slid into the seat and slammed the door.

Lethargy seeped into Marlie's muscles, leaving her motionless in a wake of sudden emotional destruction. Her mind refused to assemble any coherent thought, but created an insensible vacuum that pulled her deeper within herself. That blessed escape may have lasted an eternity if not for the call of one small voice that could penetrate the profound emptiness.

"Aunt Marlie?"

She turned slowly to Ryan, then experienced a rush of returned feelings. Until this moment she hadn't realized how much she dreaded meeting Ryan's parents. Was this reaction a dismal preface to their pending relationship? It couldn't be. But the ambivalence of enemy and friend prevailed, assimilating itself in a fear and confusion as strong as Rex Kane had ever inspired.

"Get into the truck, Ryan," she commanded him brusquely.

"But, Aunt Marlie—"

"Get into the truck! Please," she said more calmly, seeing the bewildered hurt on the child's face. "It's time to go."

With flapping cape and intelligible grumbling, Ryan did as he was told. Marlie followed, steadfastly ignoring the maroon Saab parked behind her. Once seated behind the wheel, she noticed the tools she still held in her hand. His tools. She dropped them as if they were venomous serpents.

"What's the matter, Aunt Marlie?" Ryan asked, his distress unmistakable.

Marlie mentally shook herself, trying to deny the panic that was a lit stick of dynamite tied to her composure. If she didn't get out of this alley in the next few seconds she would explode. "Nothing, darling," she said soothingly. "That nice man fixed our truck. Everything is just fine now."

Barf Dater Eliminator was on the job, defending his beloved Aunt Marlie against all injustices. "That guy wasn't nice. He was rude to you," he declared belligerently. Then slyly he added, "But I fixed him, Aunt Marlie. While he wasn't looking, I took the wind out of two of his sails for you."

Marlie stared numbly at her nephew, not knowing whether to laugh or cry. To give expression to either would certainly be inviting hysteria. For if she wasn't mistaken—and with Ryan she seldom was—the darling child had just confessed to letting the air out of two of his father's tires.

Knowing why Bryce Powell would be unavoidably detained in the alley, Marlie wasted no time in vacating the scene of Ryan's little indiscretion. She, Ryan and Happy Hanson's pickup continued on their bumpy course, and thank goodness, made it to the apartment complex before Connie and Dennis could have another parting of the ways.

By the time Marlie and Ryan entered the manager's office, Marlie had herself under control, her priorities and objectives well in hand. With Rex's threats snapping at her heels, she couldn't afford to take time out to swoon, regardless of how appealing oblivion sounded.

The manager's office compared in size and elegance to one of Stynhearst Industries broom closets. A stout woman in her late fifties reigned over a battered desk and was presently engrossed in the jigsaw puzzle spread before her.

"Mrs. Cobb?" Marlie ventured. The woman looked up. Marlie felt strangely absorbed into the gaze of warm brown eyes that reminded her of Nanny Jane's.

"Yes?"

Marlie spoke to the compelling eyes. "I was told you had an apartment for rent. We'll be here several weeks. I'm willing to pay you extra for the inconvenience of a short lease."

Mrs. Cobb got up, walked to the front of her desk and leaned against it, crossing her arms. She did her best to avoid looking at Ryan, as if the child might influence her business acumen. "I generally require at least a one-year lease, with deposits," she told the younger woman.

Marlie sighed. She had to have the *only* apartment in town, didn't she? "I'll pay you six months' rent, in cash, in advance."

Mrs. Cobb's eyebrows did an amazing volt to her graying hairline. "Who told you I had an apartment to rent?" she inquired with a trace of suspiciousness.

Marlie didn't blame the woman for wondering, but neither did she wish to answer. With little choice, she did. "Bryce Powell."

The mention of his name cleared the murky atmosphere like a spring shower. Mrs. Cobb literally beamed at Marlie—and at Ryan." Oh, well," the landlady exclaimed. "If Bryce recommends you, there's no question that you and your son will stay with me while you're in Sunnydale."

Marlie gulped. Mr. Powell hadn't exactly recommended her. Did she have to be *that* honest? Not unless Mrs. Cobb asked, she decided. She could, however, straighten out the woman on the subject of hers and Ryan's relationship. "Mrs. Cobb, I'd like you to meet my nephew, Ryan." She nudged him forward, and he shyly took the lady's hand.

"Hello, Ryan. There are several children about your age in this complex and they all seem to gather in my kitchen for homemade cookies about once a day. My apartment is over this office. We'd be pleased if you'd join us." Her offer came with the benign enthusiasm of a mother with an empty nest.

Ryan turned wide eyes on Marlie, silently asking if this lady was for real. She smiled noncommittally at the woman, for until she knew just how friendly Sunnydale was, she couldn't entrust Ryan's safety with anyone.

Mrs. Cobb didn't notice that she hadn't received an answer as she busily extracted the correct forms from a filing cabinet across the room. She returned and presented Marlie with an ink pen and a contract. Before Marlie could take them, the landlady jerked them back, a blush staining her cheeks. "Would you like to see the apartment first?"

Marlie shook her head. What was the point of looking over the only apartment in town? She signed the lease, then withdrew the appropriate funds in hundred-dollar bills from her purse. Her cash didn't faze the landlady, but apparently Marlie's signature did. Mrs. Cobb stared at the name on the dotted line a moment, then looked at Marlie, plainly trying to recollect the significance of either. Suddenly the woman's eyes widened slightly, and Marlie knew the lady was remembering where she'd come across the name Marlena Stynhearst.

Fear zinged along Marlie's nerve endings, stinging the tips of her fingers and toes, robbing her of breath. Rex Kane had been here in Sunnydale. Was he still here? Was he perhaps staying in this very complex?

Marlie feigned a laugh and selected what she hoped was a likely response. "I know what you're thinking, Mrs. Cobb," she intoned lightly. "I suspect a man was here not long ago, asking about a Marlena Stynhearst."

The landlady pouted her bottom lip. "I don't have a very good poker face, do I? He wanted to surprise you. He left a number for me to call if you showed up."

"Don't you worry, Mrs. Cobb." Marlie comforted her, with her own heart pounding in anything but comfort. "I crossed paths with the man recently, and he managed a big surprise." She pursed her lips, then asked brightly, "I forgot to ask him if he was coming back through Sunnydale, though. Did he mention anything to you?"

"He said he'd drop by to check again. That was a couple of weeks ago. He was a nice-looking man," she allowed with a hint of genial busybodiness. "Is he a business associate?"

"We work at the same Los Angeles firm, but we're on different missions that just happened to be on a possible collision course, this time," she answered.

"Well, I'm glad things worked out," Mrs. Cobb said, grabbing a set of keys from the pegboard behind her desk. "I'd hate to spoil someone's surprise."

Marlie surreptitiously sighed with relief. Rex had left Sunnydale and wouldn't return for a while. She'd bought precious time with that circuitous route across the country, but she didn't hold out much hope that Rex would give up the search for his missing victims indefinitely. After all, she had snatched his little ace in the hole from under his nose, and she had possession of a tape that would send him up the river on a very long trip. In a day or two she would have to take steps to secure more time in Sunnydale. For now, she was satisfied that Rex wasn't residing under any nearby rocks.

Marlie hadn't quite recovered from her jubilation over the outcome of this disturbing conversation with Mrs. Cobb before Mrs. Cobb was introducing another disturbing topic.

Until the landlady mentioned Bryce Powell's name again as they traversed the complex parking lot, Marlie had failed to wonder why he would know about the only vacant apartment in Sunnydale. It didn't take her long to find out. Mrs. Cobb set about informing her new tenant of every illustrious virtue characterized by Mr. Bryce Powell, another tenant.

"This will be just perfect for you, dear," Mrs. Cobb was saying. "Bryce can be a very handy man for a single woman to have around." She emitted a roguish giggle, then resumed her blithe commentary, unmindful of her companion's stoic interest. She jiggled the key in the lock, opened the door and led the parade inside, all without breaking her verbal stride.

Marlie wanted to drop a trash can over this blazing torch of information and demand the answer to one pertinent question: What about Mrs. Powell? Wasn't the lady notable enough to rate even a modest compliment? And what, for Pete's sake, was a nice woman like Mrs. Cobb doing putting a married man's services onto a public auction block?

Suddenly Marlie's jaw dropped open as a host of belated questions and speculations bombarded her. That cad in the alley, that consummation of unabashed male gall, who turned out to be Janette Powell's husband and Ryan's father, had *flirted* with her. Into what kind of family environment was she expected to leave Ryan?

Swallowing her indignation as if it were a Grand Canyon boulder, she interrupted Mrs. Cobb to ask coolly, "And how is Janette Powell doing these days?"

Marlie's question worked better than a smothering trash can; the blazing torch of information fizzled to an incredulous sputter. "Janette? Why...why Janette isn't doing too well at all, Ms. Stynhearst. She's been dead for almost two years."

Two

Bryce Powell—a thirty-four-year-old self-professed fail-ure, but with great potential for improvement—stared va-cantly out his windshield at the alley's endless expanse of potholes. He felt as he had just been clubbed over the head, dumped into one of those potholes and left for the vultures to pick clean his bones.

Happy Hanson's pickup and its two rental occupants had rattled on down the alley long ago. Soon, Bryce would have to get up the energy—or the nerve—to follow them. He didn't want to. Or maybe he did. At the moment, he wasn't too certain what was going on inside his head.

The past few months, Bryce had worked with an honest faith in success to smooth out all the wrinkles in his life. Then that woman had to come along, all bright-eyed and sassy-tongued, and towing along the one thing guaranteed to wad him up again.

Why couldn't she have been alone? Why did she have to have that fresh batch of unnerving wrinkles tagging along with her?

Bryce slammed the heel of his hand into the dash and felt the tremor clear to his brain. Good. Maybe it would shake things back into place and he wouldn't feel like going home to a bottle of spiritual consoler and celebrating his backslide into self-pity. Maybe he wouldn't be tempted to close his eyes and see again that pugnacious little rascal who had joined the woman in front of Happy Hanson's pickup. And maybe he wouldn't feel like the coward he was for walking off and leaving them puzzled by his rude behavior. The alternative would have been worse, of course. Watching a grown man shattered into a million pieces at the sight of a little boy would fluster the most unflappable.

Why wouldn't the anguish of losing his own son leave him? Bryce wondered angrily. It had been four and a half years, for heaven's sake. Almost half a decade had passed, and yet the pain still twisted in his gut from a festering wound that refused to heal.

If his son had died, perhaps Bryce and his Janette could have eventually buried the torment with their son's tiny body. But little Gordon hadn't been found dead. He hadn't been found at all. During the span of five minutes, someone had crept into their backyard and taken their eighteen-month-old son from his patio swing. The unfathomable cruelty executed in those fleeting moments had taken more from Bryce than he feared he could ever replace.

The authorities, volunteers and hired professionals, along with himself and Janette, had launched a nationwide search for Gordon. No stone was left unturned. No expense was spared. He and Janette faced financial ruin in their quest to recover their stolen child, but it hadn't been enough. In the end, after exhausting every possibility, the searchers had shaken their heads and declared the child beyond their reach.

When it was over, Bryce had lain in bed night after night, with horror stories of missing children augmenting his imagination, torturing him with visions of Gordon's probable fate. He had known that Janette lay beside him, sharing that agony, but he had been helpless to comfort her, for there had been no comfort for himself.

Painful months passed before Bryce could face acceptance of the awful truth that his son was gone. With that need to accept came a fragile hope of rallying their spirits and getting on with their lives.

Maybe that would have happened had he and Janette been given more time.

It was still difficult for Bryce to think of Janette as dead. To him, it was more like she was missing in action. Sometimes, shamefully, he was angry at her for deserting him the way she had. She should have stayed and helped him through the crushing disappointment, through the haunting dreams and shattering realities, as he had wanted to help her. People who loved each other clung to remnants of hope and together built a new future. But Janette had left him, though God knows, he didn't truly believe she wanted to. Still, she had gone to an infinite peace and left him alone to battle the demons of living.

For what seemed an eternity after her death, the demons were winning that battle. Gordon's kidnapping, Janette's death and a financially devastated air-freight company finally brought the stalwart Bryce Powell to his knees. Life had defeated him.

By day, he had buried himself in work that accomplished nothing. By night, he found solace in a bottle and the arms of an occasional woman who looked as if she could pass through his life without rousing his stymied emotions. One by one, his friends and family helplessly backed away from the frightening apparition of the man he had once been.

Then, almost a year ago, a miracle from heaven fell into his lap. The relief brought by the occasion was so immense that Bryce could actually smile at the incident now. He had been on one of his weekend self-indulgences when he woke up to find himself alone in a strange house, in a strange neighborhood somewhere in Hartford. Bemused, he had walked the streets looking for his misplaced car when he happened upon an old man who would change Bryce's life forever. Arthur Newton had said the words that finally dragged Bryce out of his apathetic haze.

Old Art had a knack for helping a man sift through the ashes of his life, showing him what was worth salvaging, what could be restored, and what should be tossed away as useless rubble. During the past months, Bryce had returned to Art's modest home to collect more of the kind man's wisdom. And lately, Bryce found himself passing on the advice at opportune moments.

These days Bryce felt as if he was a man finally healing from a long, catastrophic illness. He still had tender spots, and at times he grew weary under the strain of memories. But he was healing.

Acknowledging his fragile confidence in affairs of the heart, Bryce thought he'd found exactly what he could handle stalled in Happy Hanson's pickup. The lady's sunny disposition and whimsical sense of humor had lit up the dark corners of his heart, making her irresistible to man a who had been too long without a reason to smile.

Sunny. He didn't even know her name, but Sunny would do. Everything about her glowed. Her peachy skin, the gold and auburn highlights in her hair, the smile on her lips or the one in her eyes, all created an effect that warmed him in more ways than one. Yeah, he could have used a few nights of basking in the warmth of that petite, curving body and its dazzling accessories.

And the best thing about Sunny? She was transient. Her few weeks stay in Sunnydale wouldn't have been long enough to tempt him with an attachment that he wasn't ready to accept.

Bryce sighed with elaborate wistfulness. Sunny visiting Sunnydale—it had an almost portentous ring to it. Almost. All his great expectations had gone awry when he met her little caped traveling companion. Knowing he was being rude, hating his weakness, Bryce had, nevertheless, turned around and walked away. As much as he would have enjoyed pursuing a relationship with the woman, the child left the idea dead in his mind.

That's what you deserve for getting your hopes up, idiot. He mentally lambasted himself. *What goes up must come down.* He knew that was defeatist talk; Art Newton would shake a shaming finger at him for such thought language. Yet what else— *Honk! Honk! Honk!*

Bryce's eyes darted to the rearview mirror in a flash of annoyance. A black-and-white police car had pulled within a yard of his bumper. Grinning, he opened his door and walked over to the only law enforcement Sunnydale employed. Bracing his arms against the car door, Bryce revived his withering irritation for the sake of an old friendship. "Nickolas Vaughn, what the heck is an obvious waste of the taxpayers' money like you doing harassing a Sunnydale citizen?"

The six-foot-four-inch ex-New York police detective stuck his strikingly handsome head out the window and growled, "Bryce Powell, you couldn't catch an easy pop-fly using a bathtub for a baseball mitt, but you could catch thirty days for insulting a police officer." He motioned to the Saab. "And for illegal parking, too, runt."

Bryce smiled. "How you do go on about one lousy inch, pretty boy. I was just getting ready to move on. Had a little trouble in the alley a few minutes ago."

"Uh-huh. I saw the trouble you were having as she pulled out the other end of the alley in Happy Hanson's truck. Darn Ellie Jamison's timing. If she'd looked out her kitchen window a little sooner and reported that she thought Hap was stalled in the alley, I would've got to handle all that trouble myself."

Bryce put a hand on Nick's arm. "I spared you, Officer Vaughn, believe me," he said solemnly.

"Always thinking of others," Nick said dryly. "Well, do you want a lift to Jake's Garage or should I radio for a tow truck?"

"Why would I want either?" Bryce asked, puzzled.

Nick snickered and pointed at the Saab's left rear tire. Bryce swung his gaze in that direction, then muttered one word of the barnyard variety that summed up the situation nicely.

"Better make that a double, Bryce," Nick said, laughing, "for your trouble has come in pairs." He motioned to have a look at the other rear tire.

Already resigned to what he'd find, Bryce walked between the cars, looked, and made it a double. Unless Sunny had the talents of Houdini, there was but one person who could have sneaked back here and let the air out from his tires. Nick was right; trouble came in pairs—in varied shapes, sizes and ages.

Soundlessly, Bryce emitted a groan that came from the depths of his soul. Hadn't he been clever to point all that tribulation in the direction of his very own front door?

Veronica Cobb, Sunnydale's only landlady, was a good-natured woman who pretended to overlook a *faux pas* committed by society's ignorant. Marlie knew this because the dear lady had quickly dismissed Marlie's mortifying foolishness in inquiring about the health of a deceased woman.

Even now, twenty minutes after Mrs. Cobb had left the apartment, Marlie felt numbed by the news of Janette Powell's death. Mrs. Cobb had babbled several commiserating comments of the tragedy in poor Bryce Powell's life. Yes, Marlie agreed that losing a wife and a child would be tragic. She had lost her family, though perhaps the true tragedy had been the absence of grief of the lone survivor.

To truly empathize with Bryce Powell's circumstances, she had to think of losing the one dearest to her—Ryan. The results of this emotional exercise did nothing but create a conflict between acknowledging Mr. Powell's understandable anguish and sympathizing with her own persecutor.

At best, Marlie's position in this mess was terrible. She'd been counting on a female presence to which she could emotionally connect, for a woman would have better understood the vital importance of a child in one's life. With Janette Powell gone, Marlie was left to deal with not only a childless father but a mourning widower.

Or was she? Mrs. Cobb said Janette had died two years ago. Did inconsolable grief linger this long? Marlie replayed the scene in the alley, picturing the ruggedly handsome Bryce Powell. He had been alternately flirty and churlish. Were these stages of grief? She didn't know. What she did know was that she was being forced to befriend an unpredictable male, and thanks to her nephew's naughty gallantry in the alley, she had to start out that relationship with an apology.

What would you do, Nanny Jane? Marlie whispered to her departed friend and mentor. But Marlie knew what she would say: Do the right thing, Marlena. Do the right thing.

Marlie squeezed her eyes shut, fisted her sweaty palms and mentally rehearsed the upcoming interview with Ryan's parent. Ugh! was what she thought of the results. It wasn't very eloquent, but comprehensive and probably prophetic.

"What's the matter, Aunt Marlie? Don't you like our new apartment?"

Her eyes popped open and the fuzzy visage of her nephew dominated her view as he pressed his nose to hers. She pulled back a few inches and glanced at Ryan's attire. Thankfully, he had retired his uniform, which was absolutely necessary for the evening's remaining dubious entertainment.

"Ryan—" she began sternly.

"Not exactly our penthouse in L.A., though, is it?" The boy chattered on evasively.

"Ryan—"

"But the walls have fresh paint and the carpets are clean, aren't they? The curtains look swell. Where's the cook and the housekeeper? Are we sleeping on the floor, tonight?"

Marlie grabbed the conversation floor while Ryan took a breath. "Ryan," she commanded. "Zip it!"

Ryan knew her tone and obeyed.

Marlie took a deep breath and straightened the discouraged slump of her shoulders. "First, in brief response to your questions and excellent observations of this apartment, yes, yes, I agree, we won't have either, and probably."

The boy let out a whoop of approval, raising his fists above his head. *"Al-l ri-ight!"*

"Grab some pleasure while you can, kid. Before we camp out tonight, you are going to apologize to that man who was in the alley."

"What for?" he asked innocently.

"For taking the wind out of two of his sails. I'm on to you, Ryan B. Stynhearst. You let the air out of his tires, didn't you?"

"Yes."

For once, Marlie wished she hadn't raised the child to be so scrupulously honest. "Let's go," she ordered wearily.

"Ah, Aunt Marlie," he complained, screwing up his face in one of those scowls she didn't trust.

"Don't 'ah, Aunt Marlie' me. I'm not looking forward to facing that man again, either. I'd send you over there alone if I didn't fear he'd send back your individual body parts in little plastic bags." The prospect of physical violence amused Ryan. It didn't amuse Marlie, for she wasn't positive that she was joshing him.

According to the informative Mrs. Cobb, Bryce Powell occupied the town house two doors down. Ryan dragged his feet and Marlie dragged her spirits, but eventually the few yards separating the red brick town houses were covered. She rang the doorbell several times, then deciding that Mr. Powell must not have had enough time to change two tires, turned to leave.

Two steps down the sidewalk, she heard the door behind her burst open. She glanced over her shoulder and what she saw filling the portal described best as a modern day version of an Avenging Angel. A near-naked Avenging Angel. Bryce Powell hadn't shaved or bathed yet, but he'd removed his shoes, socks and sweaty ball jersey, and had left his pants hitched low on his hips.

All that bronzed, hair-roughened flesh might have impressed a woman who went in for that sort of thing, but at the moment Marlie was more entranced by the look in his eyes. It wasn't pleasant. Her skin prickled painfully from the darts of wrath being tossed her way by Bryce Powell's lethal gaze. Embarrassment and apprehension crowded in on her at once, making it impossible to decide how to respond to such blatant hostility.

Ryan, bless his intrepid nature, took the problem out of her hands—temporarily. "Aunt Marlie says I have to apologize to you," he told the tall, scowling man. "I will, but I'm not really sorry."

"Ryan!"

The child guilelessly looked up at his aunt. "Did you want me to lie to him?"

Yes. Yes! she silently screamed. I'm fighting to keep my life afloat and you're tossing me cement blocks. She sneaked a peak at Ryan's father—Ryan's father...that took some getting used to—and was surprised to find him lounging in his doorway, an eyebrow arrogantly cocked. No doubt he was waiting to see how she would handle this rebellion.

Frankly, she didn't have the foggiest idea of what to do about it. Except for a frightening streak of curiosity and an intolerance for intruding men, which was an attitude Marlie had come to respect, Ryan was the picture of a perfect child. How could she possibly discipline him for his honesty?

Deciding to take the bull by the horns, she grasped the smaller beast by the ear and propelled him beneath the nose of the larger. "Mr. Powell," she said gravely, "this is Ryan. As you've undoubtedly guessed, he's responsible for your delay in getting home. He *is* sorry for causing you this inconvenience, he just doesn't know it yet. But," she looked at Ryan, her meaning explicit, "he will when I get him back home."

Ryan held his ground, his furrowed brow and narrowed eyes telling Marlie that he'd take anything she dished out, but he would not be sorry. Marlie sighed and turned back to the glaring man. "Ryan sees himself as my protector," she explained ruefully.

An inexplicable expression crossed Mr. Powell's face when he glanced down at Ryan. Emotion churned the muscles of his clinched jaw until he finally dragged his eyes back to her. A steely moment passed, then the arrogant eyebrow hiked again. "And just what does the little brat think he's protecting you from?"

It took about two seconds for Mr. Powell's word choice to sink in and hit a nerve. Brat? Brat! Marlie's green eyes glittered dangerously, like shards of a broken wine bottle. Compassion and aspiring friendship fell through a trapdoor in her mind, and the stage was instantly reset for a battle scene. *Nobody* insulted her pride and joy. She met Mr. Powell's eyes with penetrating coldness and said, "From brutish men like you."

Bryce shouldered away from the doorjamb and assumed the stance of a man just itching for a good verbal tussle with a woman. "Let's back up and review the incident, lady. *I* was the victim in that alley."

From somewhere inside her, a sensible Marlie was desperately trying to coach the Marlie who wanted to kick this bully in the shin. *Friendship. Remember the objective is friendship. You* must *impress this man.*

Shoot. How she hated giving up the fight just as she was finding the courage to take on something as intimidating as the man looming over her. To surrender was reminiscent of that ugly corner Rex had backed her into only a month ago. But for the sake of the greater scheme of things, she bowed to her sensibility, hoping to do a little impressing along the way.

"Yes, you were a victim, Mr. Powell," she concurred in a voice of reason. "But not before I was. I've taught Ryan courtesy and respect. Blaring away at me with your car horn was a perfect example of rudeness. He thought I should be championed and did it the only way he knew how."

Bryce stepped out of the doorway, subtly moving in on his prey. As right as the woman was about his manners, he couldn't back off and graciously accept an apology now if his life had depended on it. That would end this encounter.

The little boy had sneaked off, and without that bittersweet hardship to endure, Bryce felt freer to pursue the pleasure at hand. Honestly, he'd hoped once he was away from this woman his initial response to her would settle into a sensible perspective and he'd forget her. But no such luck. On the contrary, she made him feel like a schoolboy again, complete with raging hormones and a downright placid intellect.

This scintillating interlude couldn't last forever, though. The child would show up again and blow a ragged hole in his desire. Until that time, Bryce could take advantage of what was available.

"Your son's sense of justice is positively frightening," he said, grinning wryly as he eased an advance along the sidewalk. "If my social infraction had been more severe, would he have slashed my tires rather than just let the air out?"

Marlie gritted her teeth. For each step he prowled forward, she measured the same distance backward. Her hopes for a mutually advantageous relationship with the man were progressing the same way. She'd reached the end of his sidewalk and retrenched behind a handy, waist-high yew a sidestep away. "Mr. Powell," she said wearily, suffering from faltering morale, "Ryan is not my son, but I've done my best as his guardian for three years."

Bryce smiled nastily. "Then perhaps his delinquent tendency is a heredity flaw, and you can find comfort in blaming the poor father."

A funny little hiccup erupted from Marlie's throat as she tried to swallow a hoot of laughter. If Mr. Powell only knew how credible his conjecture was.

With a puzzled smile, he edged around the side of the bush asking, "I said something funny?"

"Sort of," she admitted merrily, carefully maintaining a diagonal position from him. That she was being stalked wasn't lost to her, but his bush was wide and his dimples were cute, and the lightened mood was quickly reclaiming a lot of lost territory. "Will you forgive Ryan for his overzealous defenses of a favorite aunt?" she asked.

Bryce pretended to ponder her question, at the same time attempting to close the space separating them. It didn't work; she matched him inch for inch. And he was *tired* of beating around this bush. Thankful for long arms, he simply reached across the yew and snagged the woman's shoulders, whereupon reeling her in was like fighting a feisty trout.

Finally he had her where he wanted her, but she had pokered up on him. The expression on her face was empty, or perhaps frightened. "Hey, don't lose it, Sunny," he said gently. "I was just going to suggest a kiss in lieu of an apology?"

While blindly struggling, Marlie had felt only Rex's hands controlling her, remembered only her humiliating frailty yielding to his strength. But this calm, gentle voice didn't belong to Rex. Her eyes swept the length of his bare chest and upward. The smiling mouth, the enticing dimples, the intense blue eyes were not Rex's, either. "I . . . I think if you want to kiss and make up with Ryan, that would be fine."

Bryce slowly shook his head. "Not the kid. You."

Marlie's gaze fell to his bare feet. "I didn't let the air out of your tires," she murmured.

"But someone has to make retribution, and the kid's gone. So how about it?"

Her head snapped up. "Gone? Where—?" In that instant, a little black tornado tore around the yew, dodged her legs and seized her captor just above the knees. Caught unaware, Mr. Powell went down hard and fast and became buried from the belly up beneath a swirl of sateen cape.

"You leave my Aunt Marlie alone," Barf Dater Eliminator yelled. His fists were clinched, but he needed them to manage his wobbly headgear.

Marlie stuck her own fist in her mouth to hold back a wail of alarm. With eyes rounded fearfully, she watched Mr. Powell pluck the small nuisance from his chest as he bounded to his feet. He stood Ryan beside Marlie, gave her another one of his infamous scowls and promised grimly, "Later."

He stalked off toward his front door. Marlie grabbed Ryan's hand and made tracks to her own. Glad now that she'd left the door ajar for a quick escape, she shoved Ryan into the foyer. As she crossed the threshold herself, she caught a glimpse of Mr. Powell ferociously frowning her way as he leaned a naked shoulder against his closed front door. "Oh, no," she moaned, turning to Ryan. "Did you lock Mr. Powell out of his apartment?" she demanded of the grinning boy.

"Yes."

Marlie rolled her eyes heavenward. "Please, give me strength," she muttered. She slammed the front door, scolded Ryan for his devilish behavior and capped the punishment with a denied treat: no sleeping on the floor tonight. Ryan was disheartened, but not subdued. Marlie feared she hadn't seen the end of the Eliminator.

Ready to see through her threat of providing sensible sleeping provisions, she and Ryan, in Happy Hanson's reluctant transport, made a trip downtown, circumventing that dreadful alley. Connie, Dennis and the rest of the gang under the truck hood behaved while her excursion took her to a store for household accessories, a store for food and cleaning supplies and last, a furniture store. She paid cash for an entire houseful of furnishings, then stared in disbelief at the owner when he informed her it was too late to expect delivery tonight.

Marlie had never punched a time clock, but she suspected her heart wouldn't stop if she failed to punch out at five o'clock sharp. Wryly, she asked the owner if his time-sensitive employees might manage to toss her two mattresses into the truckbed. Obsequiously, he assured his customer that they could, and promised delivery of the rest of her order tomorrow.

Once back at their town house, Marlie realized her ordeal wasn't over. How was she going to get two mattresses out of the truck and up a flight of stairs? Five minutes into a wrestling match with the first mattress, which left her pinned with a smashed face to the truck rails she knew she wasn't. Not without bigger help than little Ryan.

Bigger help arrived. The mattress was plucked off her body like a speck of lint. Glancing down, Marlie recognized the bare feet of her rescuer and wondered painfully why she was shown at her worst advantage every time they crossed paths.

"Thank you, Mr. Powell," she called morosely from her side of the mattress.

"Bryce. And you're welcome," he barked back. Then he muttered, "You don't know how welcome you'd be under different circumstances."

Marlie heard his words, but didn't understand them. She didn't think she wanted to, given the wide range of possible interpretations. "Can I help you with the mattresses?" she asked tentatively.

"No."

And indeed she would have been superfluous to the task. Bryce lugged each mattress up the stairs while Marlie kept Ryan out of his way. Bryce might have appreciated her consideration, as well he should, but she couldn't be certain. The taciturn man looked at neither she nor Ryan.

The job done, her reluctant knight vanished from the premises in dramatic silence. Marlie didn't bother thanking him a second time.

Not wanting to give too much of her financial position away, Marlie opted to do her own cooking and cleaning.

This turned out to be an adventure in domestic horror. Ryan begged to help, which made two bungling housekeepers, but somehow things shaped up, with only minor calamities marking the passage of their ineptitude.

By then, the sun rested on the Sunnydale rooftops. Marlie had promised Mr. Hanson the return of his truck before dark, so after a light super, she loaded up Ryan and bounced across town to Mr. Hanson's produce corner. Happy appeared pleased to see his piece of junk home safe and sound. Chuckling to herself, Marlie surmised that this optimistic attitude was what had earned the man his name.

Thirty minutes later, Marlie and Ryan entered on foot what she'd christened Pothole Alley. It was dusk and the sporadically placed streetlights cast a gloomy pallor over the scene. Ryan, who never missed a thing no matter what the visibility, found a poor dead cat in the tall grass beside the pavement.

"I bet Mr. Powell hit him with his car," he observed implacably.

"Ryan, that's an unfair thing to say," she replied firmly, but with inward uncertain confidence.

"I still bet he did. Look how flat this kitty is. From the decomposition, I'd say Mr. Powell hit him a couple of weeks ago, and he didn't even stop to bury him."

"The sanitation department usually takes care of animal hit-and-runs, Ryan. Maybe Mr.—" She halted, realizing that she was halfway agreeing with Ryan's theory. Before she could correct that impression, headlights cut through the murky darkness. She pulled Ryan to one side of the alley to allow the vehicle by, but the vehicle stopped beside them.

Fear had no more than started percolating through her system when she recognized the maroon Saab. The passenger window descended. Bryce Powell's voice hit the warm night air like dry ice. "Get into the car."

A hundred suggestions of what he could do with his offered ride rampaged through Marlie's mind. Unfortunately, she couldn't afford the luxury of expressing any of them. She started to put Ryan in the front seat, but Mr. Powell put a stop to that notion.

"You in the front. The kid in the back. And if he pulls one trick, I'll stop the car and lash him to the bumper."

Marlie complied. And seethed. And prayed that Ryan possessed enough self-preservation to take this man at his word. She slammed her car door, pressed tightly against it and waited for the next decree to be passed down.

What came next was more on the order of an inquisition.

"What's your name?" Bryce snapped out.

"Marlie Stynhearst."

"Where are you from?"

"Los Angeles."

"Do you often take walks through dark alleys in Los Angeles?"

"No more often than I allow a strange man to order me into his car."

That shut him up. The twenty remaining potholes took a million years to traverse, but finally they reached the complex parking lot. Bryce pulled into her slot and cut the engine. Marlie didn't know what to say; "thank you" hadn't worked worth a darn in the past, so she shrugged and grasped the door handle. Mr. Powell's hand on her arm stopped her.

"I'd like to talk to you, Marlie. Privately."

Talk? Yes, they needed to talk. But this man who suffered chronic boorishness inspired such an awesome resentment in Marlie that she didn't think she could manage a conversation without wrapping her hands around his throat. She sighed, knowing she'd have to try.

Ryan reluctantly agreed to sit on the front step of their town house when she promised to be only a minute. With the child out of earshot, she turned to her obnoxious chauffeur and couldn't resist pleasantly asking, "Are you always a jerk, or is it a latent condition triggered by the presence of civility?"

For a moment, Bryce didn't know what to say; he'd never been called a jerk to his face before. Even during his bouts with the bottle, he hadn't been a mean drunk, just a pathetic one.

After his experience with the boy this afternoon, he swore to himself he'd cut a wide path around such obvious heartache. Sweet mercy, the child looked just as he imagined his Gordon would have, had he lived. The boy, Ryan, had big blue eyes, blond curly hair and a pair of dimples that would knock the girls' socks off someday. His Gordon would have, too.

But Bryce hadn't cut a wide path around anything all afternoon except his own common sense. He'd monitored the woman's activities, then butted in whenever he saw a chance. Now he was sitting in his own car, taking insults off her because, dammit, he deserved them.

"I am not a jerk, Marlie," he said irritably. "I happen to be attracted to you."

She jumped on that. A gasp prefaced her infuriated query. "You mean to tell me you've been snorting and stomping around all afternoon because you're... you're...?"

Bryce blinked in surprise. It took no imagination to fill in the blanks of her accusation. Well, well, Ms. Stynhearst, he thought, delighted with her giant leap at a wild conclusion. Even he hadn't quite narrowed down his anxieties to that indelicate distinction. But yes, sexual frustration was an acceptable excuse for his behavior. Better than admitting that he wanted her, but that her kid broke his heart.

"Yes, Marlie Stynhearst," he said matter-of-factly. "I am. So unless you're interested in going to bed with me, we have nothing else to say." He paused, then asked, "So, what do you say?"

Total silence reigned in the dark interior of the Saab. At length, Bryce nodded. "That's what I thought you'd say." He reached across her lap and released the door handle. "Goodbye, Sunny. It's been hellish knowing you."

After slamming the door with enough force to rock the Saab on its axles, Marlie stomped up her sidewalk, ordered Ryan to his feet, then applied a forced entry to her front door that any burglar would applaud. The sacks of new linen waited in the foyer. She pointed to them and instructed Ryan, "Please go make up the mattresses." Ryan, again demonstrating a remarkable sensitivity toward his aunt's moods, gathered the sacks and scatted.

Marlie plopped herself down on the bottom step, where she chewed on her opinions of Mr. Powell as if they were raw meat.

Bryce Powell wasn't stricken with grief. He wasn't embittered by loss. He was a sexually deprived Neanderthal. All those barbaric rumblings she'd heard every time they'd met had been the thump of his club and the grunt of his mating call.

Now that she thought about it, she realized that Bryce Powell's entire, consuming attention had been focused on her, not on the little boy who had left him stranded in an alley, and tackled him in his front yard and locked him out of his house. Ryan undoubtedly upset him, but it was she who was the object of his roving eye.

Being single, he was free to rove an eye over any unattached female he chose—herself included, if it made him happy—just as long as he didn't expect the compliment returned. The last time she indulged in a little roving, she tripped over her own stupidity and landed in a pack of trouble.

No, her association with Bryce Powell was going to stay on a strictly…what? Impersonal basis? Impossible. She had to make friends with that man. She had to impress that man. And at the same time, she had to manage to stay out of the bushes with that man. Assuming she accomplished those small feats, she had to mediate a relationship between father and son—another small feat, considering the son had declared war on the father.

Marlie grimaced. What a nice impression she had already made by being in charge of training the little warrior the past three years. She twisted around to frown up the staircase, the direction of Ryan's activities. "You're lucky that man chooses to ignore you, kid," she muttered.

She went upstairs, prepared to find two mattresses neatly made and Ryan ready for prayers and a bedtime story from an article in *Science Digest*. That's not what she found.

A familiar bewilderment stopped her at Ryan's door as she heard again the child's chanted words coming faintly through the wooden panel.

"Born of faith, love and joy,
My child, don't be forlorn.
Play for us your song of hope,
Upon this silver horn."

A strange little rhyme, Marlie thought. Stranger still because Ryan couldn't remember where he'd heard it, though he'd recited it numerous times in the past three years. The rhyme had, however, established a pattern of occurring during her nephew's most distressed moods.

Instantly concerned, Marlie pushed open the door and entered to find Ryan huddled in a corner of the room. "What's wrong, darling?" she asked gently, stooping beside him.

"Nothing," he muttered, though his sad little face said "everything." Marlie smiled and drew him tightly against her. "Well, if you were going to pick one thing that could be wrong, what would it be?" she asked.

Ryan's eyes swept over her face, searching. "I could be worried that you were going to leave me. But you wouldn't leave, would you, Aunt Marlie? We're going to play ball tomorrow, aren't we?"

Tears pierced Marlie's eyelids. How well she could relate to Ryan's insecurities. Swallowing, much less speaking, became a Herculean task that she had to perform. "Ryan, you can be sure if I have to go somewhere for a while, I will return to you."

"Do you promise?"

"Always," she said, and prayed that she could keep it.

Reassured, Ryan then helped Marlie prepare the mattresses and allowed himself to be tucked in for the night. Exhausted herself, she made quick but ginger use of her dubiously sanitized bathroom facilities, then aimed her body at the inviting mattress on her bedroom floor.

Dreams. Horrible dreams invaded her sleep. Fractured scenes of Ryan being wrenched from her, first by Rex, then by Bryce Powell. *"Aunt Marlie, don't leave me,"* Ryan cried. But it was too dark; she couldn't find him. She reached out, but no small body came into her arms.

She was alone. Afraid.

Marlie jerked awake, trembling, tears streaming down her face. Fear sent her fleeing to Ryan's room. A dream, just a dream, she assured herself as she knelt beside his bed. Relieved, she offered up sincere thankfulness.

"Aunt Marlie, did you have a nightmare?" Ryan whispered, his hand moving consolingly over her bent head.

Marlie looked at his sweet face, radiant in the moonlight from the window. She smiled. "Yes," she whispered back, "but I'm fine now, because you're here."

"I'll take care of you, Aunt Marlie. You don't have to be afraid."

"I know." She kissed his cheek, then went back to her bed, feeling inexplicably better.

Marlie's travel alarm clock awoke her at six o'clock the next morning. Rolling off the mattress, her feet just missed tramping on a small black bundle on the floor. A closer look revealed a sleeping Ryan, in Eliminator uniform, guarding her bedside.

In that moment, Marlie knew that she would allow nothing to separate her permanently from this child. Biology, ethicality and legality may be on Bryce Powell's side, but love was on hers. Somehow she would make that point work in her favor.

Three

Marlie, as a rule, wasn't an early riser and didn't intend to make a habit of it. But her nightmares of the night before and her not-too-successful experience with Ryan's father convinced her that today was the day to do something about gaining more time in which to improve both.

The door chimes interrupted a search through her closet for appropriate traveling apparel. She stuffed her arms into the sleeves of her silk, knee-length kimono, checked to make certain Ryan was still asleep in her bed where she'd placed him, then trotted down the stairs. Who could be calling at this hour? Assuming the worst, she took a cautious peek through the hole in the door. It wasn't Rex; maybe it was worse. Mr. Powell stood on her doorstep, looking very good in his gray pin-striped suit and red silk tie, but otherwise as grim as ever.

She opened the door and tried to smile at him. "Good morning, Mr. Powell."

"Bryce. And I disagree, Marlie." His lips twisted dourly. "My good morning fell apart when I took the garbage out."

"Oh?"

"Mmm-hmm. Imagine my dismay at finding a dead cat in my trash can."

"Oooh."

"That wasn't exactly what I said, but I see you get my point."

Marlie slumped dejectedly against the doorjamb, unaware that her new position allowed her kimono to expose an unseemly amount of leg and chest. Bryce noticed, though. What he could see matched the mental picture of her body that he had been carrying with him since last night. He hadn't slept a wink because of it, and now his disposition felt as if it had a blister rubbed on it. "Why me?" he demanded of no one in particular.

Knowing he expected her to explain, Marlie said, "The cat in your trash can was the result of a misunderstanding. I told Ryan that the sanitation department disposes of dead animals. But the cat had been ignored, and because Ryan is a sweet, compassionate child, he took care of the problem himself."

Sweet and compassionate? Bryce stared at her a moment in disbelief, then with polite nastiness said, "You've heard the old saying, good fences make good neighbors, Marlie? If I have to, I'll build another Great Wall of China around my property to keep that sweet and compassionate nephew of yours out. If that doesn't work, I'll have to assume this is some cunning act you've devised to catch a father for the kid and a husband for yourself."

Whap!

Bryce rubbed his stinging cheek. Damn, but she had a fast reaction time. She had a wicked mouth on her, too, when it came to defending that kid. Her tirade meant to sting his ears, as her palm had stung his cheek. Moments passed and Marlie showed no sign of running down. Deciding to see what other wicked things her mouth could do, Bryce abruptly pulled her into his arms and terminated his verbal crucifixion with his own mouth.

Marlie struggled but he hung on, first demanding a shared desire, then sweetly cajoling her with light, playful caresses. As his kiss altered from subjugation to persuasion, so did her response. She softened and hesitantly participated in what was for him a quite pleasant event.

When the kiss ended, Bryce noted that she wasn't exactly overcome with reciprocated lust, but neither was she slapping his face again. He reluctantly let her go, not knowing whether he had won or lost this confrontation.

Marlie shared his confusion. His kiss had confounded her. She liked it; she hated it. She wanted to kiss him again to help make up her mind. She wouldn't, of course. His caress had lacked the violence she associated with Rex, but Mr. Powell had just demonstrated that he wasn't averse to using a little masculine power and an irresistible magnetism to get what he wanted.

As for his horrible accusation, it had angered her. Yes, she was trying to catch Ryan a father. But a man for herself—absolutely not! She was willing to give up a lot to keep Ryan safe, to return him to his rightful place, but she didn't feel obliged to sacrifice her self-respect. Mr. Powell had stepped over the line with his crude remark, and whether or not she had forfeited ground in their relationship with her equally crude retaliation, she refused to regret her actions. Rex's physical and emotional manipulations still doused her dignity with scalding humiliation, and she promised herself that it would be a long time before she'd submit to the dominance of another man.

She looked up into a handsome face that mirrored some curiosity, some regret and a lot of passion. The passion had to go, for practical purposes. Quietly she said, "You're off the hook, Mr. Powell. If I was looking for a husband, I wouldn't settle for an ape in a business suit."

Bryce's lips twitched with amusement. "Bryce. And I deserve the insult, along with the slap. Rest assured, three loosened jaw teeth has shown me the error of my ways." He took a step back and gave her a lopsided smile. "So long, Marlie. I'll pray that the kid doesn't turn on you in the future."

Marlie watched him go, worried. He seemed to think they were parting ways on this doorstep, but he was wrong. They would meet again, and the encounters would be complicated by an unnecessary sexual attraction. Why did he have to muddle their relationship with sex? she wondered dismally. She couldn't allow it to happen, and she wouldn't explain to him why.

Ryan came bouncing down the stairs, interrupting her rumination. He threw his sturdy little arms around her, greeted her with a perky "Good morning" and sloppy kiss on the cheek.

"I love you, Aunt Marlie," he said, sitting down beside her on the step.

Marlie sighed. "I love you, too, though I suspect you're a troublemaker."

"Am I a troublemaker?" he asked, not too disturbed by the possibility.

"Probably," she said, grinning. "I'd go broke having your motives analyzed. For instance, Mr. Powell just stopped by on his way to work. He told me about the distressing experience he had, taking out his trash this morning."

Ryan stared at his bare toes poking out the bottoms of his pajamas, but he didn't comment.

Marlie refused to talk down to Ryan. He was young but smart, and he asked questions when he didn't understand. Out of respect for his intelligence she gave it to him straight. "I'm going to choose to believe that what you did was done out of compassion for the cat," she told him gently. "If your motive was otherwise, you should be ashamed of yourself. That said, I want your promise that you will never sneak off at night again."

"Ah, Aunt Marlie, I know better than to talk to strangers, and I watched for cars."

Yes, but did you watch for Rex Kane? she wondered uneasily. "Promise me, Ryan." Her command was unyielding.

"Okay," he conceded, perturbed but resigned.

She sighed gratefully, knowing she could trust Ryan with a pinpoint precise agreement. She cuddled him closer, took a deep breath and broached a subject that she knew wouldn't thrill him any more than it did her. "Ryan, I've got some business to take care of today and I can't take you with me."

"What kind of business, Aunt Marlie? Why can't I go, too?"

"You can't go because you'd need a passport." When he was about to argue, she cut him off, explaining, "I'll be gone just for the day, I promise. If Mrs. Cobb agrees to keep you, maybe she'll let you help her make cookies." Her smile was calculated. "That'll be a new experience for you. One you won't likely get with me." It worked. Marlie watched as Ryan thought through the intriguing process of taking several ingredients and producing one product and became hooked on the idea.

Thankfully, Mrs. Cobb was, too. Marlie invested considerable anxiety over the decision to leave Ryan with a stranger, but it had to be done, and Mrs. Cobb was the best choice of unknown candidates. The landlady waved away all Marlie's apologies for the imposition and looked insulted by the offer of money. As if that wasn't enough, she refused Marlie's request to call and cancel the furniture order and instead volunteered to be on hand to supervise the delivery. With everything settled, Mrs. Cobb shooed Marlie out the door with one hand while guiding Ryan to the kitchen with the other.

It was the start of an entire mission blessed with perfection. At exactly 2:00 p.m. Marlie walked into the Bank of Winnipeg and opened a modest checking account with funds transferred from her bank in Los Angeles. As an afterthought, she went shopping, freely using her credit cards. As she was establishing herself as a new resident in the Canadian city, she knew Rex would be closely monitoring her L.A. bank account for transaction activity in hopes of locating her.

Let Rex track her here and turn Winnipeg upside down looking for her, she thought with wicked vindictiveness. Her only regret was that she wouldn't be around to watch his frustration mount.

She boarded her home-bound plane at five o'clock that evening, exhausted but elated. Hopefully, she had gained enough time to see Ryan safely settled in his rightful place, and a place for herself with him . . . if Ryan, in his unmitigated guardianship, didn't mutilate all likelihood of this happening.

Ryan's happy face flashed in her mind, and for the first time since kissing him goodbye that morning, she allowed thoughts of the child to invade her purpose. How had he and Mrs. Cobb fared? she wondered wistfully.

Actually, Mrs. Cobb and Ryan had fared wonderfully together until Mrs. Cobb received an urgent call from an ailing friend across town. It was early evening, Ms. Stynhearst wouldn't return for hours and a sickroom was no place for a little boy. What to do? Mrs. Cobb wondered frantically. Suddenly the perfect solution came to her: Bryce Powell. He could take care of an energetic little boy. Within minutes she had Ryan and his duffel bag gathered and deposited on the doorstep of the child's favorite victim.

Bryce answered the doorbell on the second ring and stared in open dismay at his visitors. Before he could oppose the invasion, his landlady had pushed the boy over his threshold and launched her persuasion speech. "Dear Bryce, thank goodness you're home. I was at my wit's end, worrying what to do with sweet little Ryan here. Mildred Smith's back is out again, poor thing, and I simply must go to her. Be a sweetheart and watch Ryan until Ms. Stynhearst returns. Ryan has the keys to their apartment if you need anything. Otherwise, I've left her a note on the door. She'll know where to look. Thanks again, you dear man. Ta ta."

And that was it. Bryce stared, slack-jawed, as the night swallowed up the perpetrator of this nightmare.

Bryce clenched his teeth against the unfairness of fate as he motioned the boy to follow. He'd put a movie in the VCR that they could both watch, then ignore the child until his aunt picked him up. With any luck, a whole evening could pass without having his heart stomped by an uncaring little squirt who had the nerve to remind Bryce too much of the joys of fatherhood that he was missing with his own son.

According to plan, Bryce filled a small bowl with popcorn and placed it, along with a cola, on the coffee table, then stretched out on the sofa with his own popcorn bowl balanced on his hip. The movie feature he chose was three hours long; if Marlie didn't come by the end of the show, he'd rewind the blasted thing and they'd watch it again.

This great plan may have worked if Ryan hadn't made plans of his own. Not the least bit interested in a dumb old war movie, he donned his uniform in the bathroom, loaded his weapon and sneaked into position. Fortuitously timed with a bombing raid on the TV screen, Ryan popped up from behind the sofa and shot Mr. Powell three times in the left ear with his water pistol. "Take that, you barf dater," he shouted triumphantly.

Bryce exploded off the sofa amid a shower of popcorn. For a stunned moment, he didn't know what had hit him. The water pistol in the hands of his weirdly dressed little visitor gave him a clue. Without giving himself time to think, he snatched the kid up and plopped him down on the kitchen bar that separated the rooms. From this level, it seemed more like talking to an adult. He spoiled the effect by growling, "How would you like a good spanking for that trick, kid?"

Ryan's chin came up and his top lip sank behind his bottom one. He looked like a tenacious little bulldog contemplating the mailman's leg. *You're going to rip my heart to shreds, aren't you, kid?* Bryce thought in morose wonder. For even while water yet dripped from his left ear, Bryce had to admire the boy's bravery.

"That's an illogical question," Ryan informed him scornfully. "No kid likes a spanking and there's no such thing as a good one, sir."

Sir? Somehow Bryce felt intimidated by the respectful title. He avoided the short, rhythmic swinging legs and disarmed the ruffian, then removed his helmet and glasses. "Illogical or not, do you get my message?" he demanded.

"Yes, sir. You don't want me to shoot you in the left ear anymore."

"Or the right ear," he added, thinking to cover all bases with this cute conniver. Then, curious despite himself, he asked, "Why do you do this to me?"

"Because you want my Aunt Marlie."

"How do you know?" he demanded incredulously. This was a kid, for Pete's sake.

"Because you look at her."

"So? Your Aunt Marlie's nice to look at."

Ryan nodded. "I know. She smells good, too."

"I wouldn't know about that. She doesn't like me to get that close."

"She does Rex."

Did Bryce truly want to know? Apparently. "Who's Rex?"

"Another barf dater. I tried to tell Aunt Marlie that he's a creep—" Ryan sighed dejectedly "—but she still engaged him."

"What do you mean, she engaged him?" Bryce asked ominously.

Ryan rolled his eyes impatiently. "They're getting married."

Bryce winced, taking an unexpected punch in the gut. "Are you sure?" he rasped.

"Well—" the boy leaned forward, anxious to confide his great secret "—the day before we left L.A. I smeared Limburger cheese on the manifold of Rex's car. That probably took care of the problem."

Bryce blanched and felt a spurt of pity for the unfortunate Rex. As for Marlie's engagement, he decided to take this news with a grain of salt. She didn't act engaged.

Heaving a great sigh, Bryce stared at the kid on his bar who could have been a clone of his own lost child. Physically, that is, he hastily amended. No child of his would have behaved like this one. "How are old you? Eight or nine?" he asked abruptly.

"Six, sir."

"You're pretty smart for a six-year-old."

"Yes, sir. I'm a genius," he said forlornly, then brightened. "But Aunt Marlie's helping me with the problem."

Bryce didn't even want to get into how Aunt Marlie could alleviate genius. He didn't doubt that she could, though, for she was certainly doing a number on *his* mental acuity. Ryan or no Ryan, he wanted Marlie in a way that seriously undermined every moral, every principle, every speck of wisdom that he professed to claim.

He defined part of his grievance as pure jealousy of a woman who had won a child by default, when he had lost his child by defeat. This tedious self-analysis wasn't improving his temper, for he was fed up with the results. Fed up with his anger and frustration and fed up with feeling like a fool for allowing a little boy to scare him away from something he wanted.

In a few weeks Marlie would be gone, and he would have missed all the good things that might have happened. He needed a dose of her spunky temperament, and he refused to be denied the pleasure of showing Marlie that she'd enjoy his company as much as he'd enjoy hers.

One way or another, the child was a fact of life to be endured, so why not make this forced confinement work in Bryce's favor? "Ryan," he said, man-to-man. "You're right about me wanting your Aunt Marlie. But I'm not like that creep, Rex, because I don't want Marlie to engage me." Not the way Ryan meant, anyway, he added mentally. "So you see, I would be a safer—" He groped for a word, which Ryan supplied.

"Barf dater?"

Bryce scowled and didn't deign to agree.

Ryan got a gleam in his eye that his Aunt Marlie would have instantly recognized. With no one around to warn this poor guy, Ryan considered him fair game. "I take you for a sporting man, sir," the boy said, giving his best salesman pitch. "So here's what I propose. A contest. If I win, you stay away from my Aunt Marlie. If you win, you can try to date her without my interference."

Bryce shook his head, marveling at the kid's temerity.

"Oh, come on, sir, I'm just a little kid. You're supposed to indulge me. Pleeease."

Bryce shrugged. Why not? The boy had to learn better sometime. "All right. Since you're just a little kid and need indulging, I'll take you up on your challenge. To make this fair, you can chose the contest."

"Video games," the child responded without hesitation.

"Okay. You have any?"

"Sure."

They trooped over to Ryan's apartment where Ryan spread out an impressive collection of games for Bryce's perusal. Bryce selected one that he had at least heard of. While Ryan raided the refrigerator, Bryce was granted a warm-up. "A piece of cake," he muttered, greatly self-assured, fifteen minutes later.

Two hours later, Bryce was sweating profusely. The kid was an outstanding player and Bryce was down ten thousand points. He saw his goal slipping through his fingers. Then he mentally pictured said goal and felt renewed determination.

Marlie entered her apartment a little after nine that night and came face-to-face with a sight that floored her—a smiling Bryce Powell standing beside a frowning Ryan. In fact, Ryan looked as if the bottom had just dropped out of his world. "What's wrong, Ryan?" she demanded, shooting an accusing glance at Mr. Powell.

"I lost you, Aunt Marlie," he said disconsolately.

Marlie swallowed heavily. With foreboding, she looked at Bryce, but asked Ryan, "How did you lose me?"

"Battling Baboons," the boy confessed, shamefaced. "Mr. Powell won, and now he gets to date you."

To say Marlie was shocked at this turn of events would have been an overdose in understatement. Ryan led his aunt to the sofa and solicitously asked if she'd like something to drink.

"Double Scotch, on the rocks," muttered a woman who had been a teetotaler all her life.

"We don't keep alcoholic beverages, Aunt Marlie," the child reminded her worriedly.

"She doesn't need booze, Ryan," Bryce interjected, a satanical smile if Marlie ever saw one twisting his lips. "She's just momentarily overcome by the joyful prospect of going out with me. It's a common reaction with the women I date."

Marlie shot him a withering glance. "I will not go out with you," she said succinctly.

"But, Aunt Marlie, you've got to," Ryan exclaimed. "I'll be a welsher, if you don't. You don't want me to be a welsher, do you?"

Bryce kept smiling. Marlie had an unholy urge to indent those dimples of his a little deeper with her fist. "It's time for you to go to bed, Ryan," she said levelly. When he would have squawked, she gave him one of her looks that sent him quietly on his way.

Alone with her prospective date, she nervously walked to the sliding doors overlooking the patio and stared into the night. Bryce allowed her to stew a few minutes, then came up behind her to wrap her loosely in his arms.

"I don't have two heads and seldom breathe real fire," he said softly. "Why is a date such a big deal?"

Marlie wanted to leap out of his tender grasp, and at the same time burrow more deeply into it. Too mixed-up to think of a sensible reason, she settled for a pitiful excuse. "It just won't work."

He gave her a little hug that brought her closer. She did smell wonderful, like spring flowers after a rain. "How do you know it won't work if you don't give it a try?"

A small, unguarded chuckle escaped. "I don't have to try sticking my elbow in my ear to know that won't work, either." She peered over her shoulder at him, her expression perplexed. "I slapped your face, for Pete's sake. Why would you want to date me?"

Bryce grinned. "Beats me. I guess I kind of like a tough woman who's on a first name-basis with auto parts."

She smiled weakly. "I can't go out with you, Mr. Powell. Not on a date."

"Bryce. And you're annihilating my vanity, dear. But that aside, Ryan's not going to take it kindly if you make him renege, and neither am I." Marlie still looked as if she had an itch she couldn't scratch. He supposed he knew why. "I didn't show much finesse when I propositioned you the other night, Marlie. Under normal circumstances I hardly ever ask a woman to bed with me before I ask her to dinner. In your case, proper order is even more imperative, considering your nephew's attitude toward male competition." He smiled. "I shudder to think what might happen if we got caught sharing the same sheets."

Getting caught didn't worry Marlie nearly as much as being in the position to get caught. Bryce Powell was attractive, no point in denying it. Kissing him had been more than pleasant, though she refused to give him a rating. Rex had also been good-looking and an adequate kisser, though in the end, both had amounted to a diddle in their relationship. No more being led astray by tactile attributes, right, Stynhearst?

"I shudder to think about that, too, Mr. Powell," she agreed stoutly. "Maybe we should settle for something a bit more restrained."

"Like what?" he asked, indulging her with a pretense of interest as he turned her around to face him.

Marlie's gaze slid from his face to his chest. "How about friendship?"

"Is that less dangerous?"

She closed her eyes briefly, allowing a unchallenged wave of disappointment to wash over her, then said flatly, "Yes, Mr. Powell. Friendship offers far less peril to both our well-being."

"*Bryce*," he enunciated. "If you call me Mr. Powell again, I might have to breathe some fire. As to your observation on peril, obviously I can't disagree. But male fantasies die hard, Marlie. When I envision myself chatting in the backyard with my pretty chum, there's something missing from the picture."

"It's the fence," she proposed curtly. "You threatened to build one, and you're doing a fine job of it."

Bryce picked up a brunette curl laying enticingly on her breast. The silky strands wrapped around his finger, clinging to him as he wished the rest of her would feel inclined to do. "No more fences. Go out with me."

Marlie fretted, boxed in by her hard-won wisdom. Soon, very soon, she would be turning over her most precious possession into this man's care. Intimate involvement with Ryan's father would be suicide to a sensible, long-term relation. "Couldn't we *try* being just friends, Bryce?" she asked, using his given name to highlight her willingness to trend in a friendly direction.

"Oh, we could try anything, Marlie. The question is whether I would live through it. If I'm to sacrifice myself for a woman, I'd like to know I went with at least a smile on my face."

Marlie swallowed a reluctant laugh. Bryce had a valid fear. She knew she wouldn't tangle with Ryan in a protective mood. But Ryan couldn't keep her safe forever. It wasn't a question of wanting, but needing, to meet this man on some kind of common ground. With the deck reshuffled, she had to rethink her strategy, for a date hadn't been part of it.

Okay, she thought, resigned. No big deal. "To save Ryan's reputation, I'll go with you to a park for a little sightseeing tomorrow afternoon."

"Sorry, Sunny," he said. "I'm a working stiff. I haven't had a Saturday off since my great depression." Holding on to her arms so she couldn't get away, he added, "I'll pick you up at four o'clock, and we'll do a little sightseeing, eat, then . . . we'll see. Okay?"

"I suppose it's pointless to mention that I have a little boy and no baby-sitter," she said in a voice of mostly decayed patience.

"I'll get the sitter. Mrs. Cobb owes me a huge favor," Bryce said sardonically, digging in his heels when Marlie would shove him out the door. He wasn't to be rushed. He tugged her into his embrace, wrangled a lip alignment and kissed her. When he finished exploring the possibilities of her limited participation, he let her go, grinning knowingly. "I'll see you tomorrow at four," he said, and left.

Alone, Marlie slumped against the wall and stared at the toes of her black patent pumps. Sometimes it was a disadvantage knowing oneself so well. Marlie did, so it made her accountable for her behavior. A woman raised without a loving family tended to seek affection where available, and Marlie was no exception. In defense of her virtue, she had devised a moderated code of frigidity, a frigidity born of caution, not indifference.

Through the years, the male half of Marlie's sophisticated acquaintances had shown her a thing or two about the art of kissing, even kissing of the French influence, with a focus on greater intimacy. And through those same years,

Marlie had shown those same male companions a thing or two about the art of saying no, and meaning it.

With Bryce, she wanted to show off her binational expertise. With Bryce, she wanted to say yes. She had fought it; with all her assumed frigidity, she had fought it. She had kept her lips firmly sealed against another sophisticated invasion, and triumphed—barely.

But what about the next time?

Of all men, why did Bryce Powell have the power to corrupt her carefully controlled libido?

No answers were written on the toes of her pumps. Dispirited, she gathered up strength and finally made it up the stairs to Ryan's door. She pressed an ear to the panel, heard the mysterious rhyme being softly chanted and entered the room to find Ryan crouched in the corner. She joined him there and asked the standard question, "What's wrong?"

Ryan shrugged and offered her his standard answer, "Nothing." But the tears welling in his eyes made a fibber out of him. Needing her reassurance much more than he feared her anger, he looked up at her and asked, "You aren't real mad at me for losing you in that game, are you, Aunt Marlie?"

Marlie sighed heavily. "Well, I can't say that I'm exactly overjoyed at being gambled away. What made you do such a thing?"

"I thought I could beat him. Then he'd stay away from you. But I lost, and now I have to let him have you."

"He can't have me, Ryan," she said firmly. "I'll go on one date with him, which is all your fault. But that's all."

"Do you promise, Aunt Marlie? You won't ever leave me, will you?" He pressed her cheeks within his small hands and tugged her desperately closer. "You have to teach me to throw a ball and all the other things real boys do. I can't start first grade without knowing that stuff."

Marlie wrapped her arms around his squirming body and rocked him like the child he was. Genius carried its own burden that only another of like intellect could truly understand. Most children were taught to be students; Ryan was a student wanting to be a child. He so anxiously wanted to be like other children, but he often didn't understand them, nor they him.

How well Marlie understood his fear of rejection. Learning the games that children play had been the compromise he had accepted in order to become one of them. Teaching him the games had been the challenge she had accepted on his behalf.

"I'll not let you down, sport," she promised softly. "We're a team, remember? We need each other."

Ryan nodded against her chest, and with his assurance renewed, he climbed into bed. Marlie turned out the light and smoothed his blond curls as he drifted off to sleep, while silent tears slipped down her cheeks. She didn't believe that anyone, not even a father, could love Ryan more than she. But her love for Ryan didn't count. Her need for Ryan didn't count. And least of all, her want of Ryan didn't count. What counted was that Ryan belonged to someone else, a man Marlie couldn't even say she liked. But that didn't count either.

Saturday dawned with a gloomy temperament, but grudgingly gave way to modest sunshine by four o'clock. Marlie and Ryan, both dressed in jeans and T-shirts, were waiting at the Saab when a grim-faced Bryce joined them, similarly attired.

"You're obviously a slave to your emotions, Bryce Powell," Marlie commented, determined to put a happy face on this error in judgment. "One moment you're acting almost human, complete with smile. The next, well..."

"I'm always human, Marlie Stynhearst, as you will soon find out. The only thing I'm a slave to is other people's wholehearted endeavor to screw up my plans." He motioned to Ryan. "We'll have a short chaperon until Mrs. Cobb returns from another one of her mercy missions."

Bryce was the only one vexed with this unexpected reprieve. Ryan piled into the back seat of the Saab while Marlie leapt lightly into the front. Bryce followed more sedately, frowning. "Don't get too high on relief, dear," he growled sotto voce as he leaned in her direction to wiggle the car keys from his pocket. "Mrs. Cobb will be back in a couple of hours, then the rest of the night will be ours alone.''

Marlie smiled her most insincere smile. "Don't threaten me, Bryce," she whispered back. "I didn't lose at Battling Baboons, and I'm here to humor a little boy, not a big one.''

Bryce's returned smile *was* boyish, his dimples dotting the exclamation of amusement in his blue eyes. "We'll venture into the difference between little boys and big boys when your loaded pistol isn't aimed at the back of my head," he said, motioning toward Ryan.

Marlie had decided not to allow Bryce to buy her dinner, for she remembered what he'd said could come after a meal the last time they had discussed the proper order of these things. That was why the delicious roast beef sandwich and home-fried potatoes Bryce insisted on feeding her kept backwashing through her digestive system.

Over lemon meringue pie, Bryce brought her up to date on an old farmhouse he was having remodeled and the need to make a quick trip out to it to check on the progress.

"I'd like to see your new house," she said promptly, hoping that seeing where Ryan would be living would make it easier for her to let him go.

Bryce looked surprised, but not displeased with her eagerness. He paid the bill, giving her a dirty look when she insisted she would pay for hers and Ryan's meals. "Call me old-fashioned, but when I ask a woman out, I expect to pay for it, Marlie," he growled.

"But—"

He croaked a finger to beckon her, and when she met him halfway over the table, he whispered in her ear, "Hush."

Marlie hushed and left for the car in a huff. Turning Ryan over to Bryce for the remainder of the child's formative years was a sobering thought. Just what the female half of the population needed: a father-and-son duo of harmonized male chauvinism.

Her mood lightened during the short drive to Bryce's house as the pastoral beauty of the landscape whizzed by her open window. Rolling fields and meadows lay in patches of green and brown, seamed together with endless lines of age-old rock fences. Ryan commentated on the trip, comparing the roadside trees and wildflowers with pictures he'd seen in books, and very likely, in his own mind given his extraordinary memory retention.

Within minutes from town, Bryce was turning onto a long, gently ascending gravel drive. When they reached the top, the surrounding countryside stretched before them. Sunnydale lay in the valley below them, scattered amid the green foliage like colorful veggies in a salad bowl. In wonder, Marlie stared at Bryce's restored farmhouse. It could have sprouted from the rich earth, so perfect was its setting. "Your home is beautiful, Bryce," she said simply.

Bryce looked at the traditional two-story, painted white with forest-green shutters, seeing what Marlie saw, but differently. He and Janette had purchased this house and land six months before their son's birth, with kids and dogs and wide open spaces for romping in mind. After Gordon's disappearance, Janette lost interest in remodeling the house; they never lived in it.

Bryce still thought often of Janette and Gordon and the dreams that might have been, though mourning them had finally ended. He could appreciate the fond memories of the past, then release them, like a pristine snowfall yields its beauty to the warmth of a promising sun.

This house had stood waiting for two years, silently offering Bryce a chance to bring him contentment. A few months ago, he decided to grant himself that chance.

Standing on the wraparound porch, Bryce pointed west over the tops of towering elms, poplars and beeches, and told Marlie, "Hartford's about twenty miles from here. AirShip Freight has a landing strip, hangars, office and warehouse at a private airport east of Hartford."

"AirShip? Is that where you put in your time as a working stiff?"

He grinned. "Yeah. It's been an interesting challenge to resurrect a doomed company, but it seems to be happening slowly but surely. You are talking to the lock, stock, and barrel owner of Powell's AirShip Freighting Company, dear. The rewards and the headaches are mine, all mine."

Financial assistance could be a way for Marlie to insinuate herself within the Powell domain. Carefully, she negotiated the tricky waters ahead. "Was it poor economy that effected your business adversely?"

For a moment Bryce watched Ryan and a neighbor's golden retriever romp happily on the green terraced lawn as he wondered how to answer her question. There were no secrets in this little town; everyone knew most of the circumstances of Bryce Powell hitting the skids two years ago. Anyone Marlie cared to ask could tell her all about it—if they hadn't already. Why not be honest?

Taking advantage of their privacy, Bryce led Marlie to a bench swing at the end of the porch. "No, Marlie, it wasn't poor economy, it was self-pity that nearly finished off AirShip," he confessed, picking up her hand and lacing his fingers with hers. "You're very politely tiptoeing around the rumors that I'm sure you've heard. I'll give it to you first-hand, so you won't have to wonder."

He nudged the swing into gentle motion and began relating as much as he could bear of the most miserable time in his life. When he finished, he turned to her. "I lost it, Marlie. I couldn't handle it, so I made friends with a bottle and tried drinking myself into oblivion. Then I made friends with someone who had something better to offer, and things have been improving ever since."

Marlie's chest heaved with the effort of drawing breath through a constricted windpipe. She should ask him questions; it was the natural thing to do since he'd opened the conversation. But she didn't want to know the details of his life with Janette, or the details of Ryan, which she probably knew better than Bryce did. Rather, she should be the one sharing Ryan's past with his father, the years that should have been his, but had been mercifully diverted to her. Bryce's loss had been her gain, and she at least owed him a tour by imagination through the precious years he'd missed.

You should tell him now, she thought wretchedly. Tell him that all wasn't lost, that he has a son, and things can improve even more. But she couldn't push those words out. Instead, she muttered the generically appropriate words of a sympathetic stranger and left her conscience unappeased.

Bryce smiled at Marlie, feeling a strange comfort from baring his soul to her. He abandoned the swing, pulling

Marlie up with him. "Come on," he said briskly. "Let's look at the house. I didn't bring you out here to cry on your shoulder."

Marlie nodded, but offered no comment as she followed him inside. The front door opened into a large, airy living room. A huge stone fireplace extended the length of one wall, a long oak staircase another. A few boxes sat on the hardwood floor of the otherwise barren room. Bryce glanced at the boxes, then quickly away. "They're filled with memorabilia," he said woodenly. "They'll go in the attic when I have time."

Bryce showed her through all ten rooms of the house, each one bare of any adornment. "I'm not much of a hand at decorating. Right now I'm not worried about the niceties, just privacy and some peace," he explained.

Again she offered no comment. Time was pressing upon her, and she knew she must open the conversation of his missing son. Tonight? Tomorrow? Would waiting a few more days be so wrong? She followed Bryce back downstairs, vacillating between telling him now, later or possibly never, which kept creeping in as she silently rehearsed her confession.

In the end, the decision was not hers to make.

Ryan, with his typical curiosity, had entered the house and was presently sneaking a peek into those boxes on the living room floor. In his exploration, he'd discovered a small silver horn. Marlie and Bryce had reached the bottom of the staircase just as Ryan began to chant.

"Born of faith, love and joy,
My child, don't be forlorn.
Play for us your song of hope,
Upon this silver horn."

Marlie thought nothing of the child relating the rhyme to the little instrument in hand, until she looked at the expression on Bryce's face. The man looked as if he'd been turned to stone.

Four

———

"**D**ear Lord," Marlie whispered. For now she knew where Ryan had learned the rhyme. Before she could do anything, Bryce lunged at Ryan, grasping his arms, shaking him.

"Where did you hear that rhyme?" he shouted at the child.

Ryan looked at Marlie, too frightened and bewildered to answer. She rushed to Bryce's side and pulled against the vise of his hands. "Bryce," she murmured frantically, "you're terrifying the child. Please, let him go. I can tell you what you want to know."

Slowly her words penetrated his conscience, and Bryce released the boy. He straightened and looked at her, a maelstrom of emotions in his eyes. Finally a shudder ripped through his body, releasing him from a terrible spell cast by the resurged past.

The child had wrapped his arms around Marlie's waist and turned his face away from Bryce. "I'm sorry," Bryce muttered, still slightly disoriented by his loss of control. He had frightened the child, and unintentional though it was, he felt badly. He knelt on one knee beside the boy and patted his trembling shoulders. "I didn't mean to scare you, Ryan. Did I hurt you?"

Ryan cautiously turned to Bryce, his face still white. "N-No," he stammered.

Marlie pulled Ryan away from her and gave him a hard-earned smile. "Why don't you go outside and wait for me on the porch swing? Mr. Powell and I need to talk."

Ryan quickly consented, not that she believed for a second he wouldn't. She wanted to run, too, for the moment of truth had arrived. Before she could begin to tell Bryce the news she had been saving for weeks, he was speaking.

"I didn't mean to lose control like that," he said, running forked fingers through his hair in agitation. "When I heard Ryan recite that poem, I went nuts." He shoved his hands into his pockets, walked over to a window and stared out. "I need to talk to him, Marlie," he said more calmly than he felt. "That little horn he found belonged to my son. The poem he was reciting was taught to Gordon by his mother. If Ryan can remember where he heard the poem, there may again be hope of finding my child."

Marlie cleared her throat. Fear twisted her fingers together into painful knots. Her words came out like deeply rooted wisdom teeth. "You've already found him, Bryce."

She thought she'd prepared herself for any reaction from Bryce, but she hadn't. He stiffened, as if her words were vicious blades driven into his back. He slowly turned to her, his face wiped clean of expression. "What did you say?" he asked.

"Ryan is your son, Bryce. I've brought him back to you."

Bryce seemed to explode at her from across the room, one moment a rock of impenetrable stillness, the next, a rush of intensely heated ire. His hands gripped her arms until her bones ached. His face pressed near hers, a mask of ugly accusations and disbelief. "You're lying," he snarled.

Fear writhed in the pit of her stomach. Yet, with vivid clarity, she understood and sympathized with his contradicting emotions. Bryce was afraid to believe. She touched his face with gentle fingertips, instilling a sense of reality to her words. "He's alive, Bryce. Ryan is your son."

He let her go then, and she watched as he assessed her words, applying logic and order to chaotic perceptions. Mere seconds measured the degrees of his returning composure.

"I think you have a lot to tell me, Marlie Stynhearst," he said, almost serenely. "We'll start with the easy stuff. Who are you?"

Marlie began to relax. The worst was over; she could reason with him now. "I'm Marlena Stynhearst. Ryan started calling me Marlie when he first came to me."

A muscle twitched along Bryce's jaw. "You and Ryan have been living in Los Angeles all these years?"

"For three years. He's been with me since my brother and his wife were killed in a accident. Bryce—"

"Did you know how your brother and his wife went about getting this child?"

"No. Not at first, but—"

"I'll admit that the boy with you does have a striking resemblance to Gordon," he said casually. "The age fits, and certainly reciting the poem adds authenticity. How much do you want for the kid?"

Marlie drew in a sharp breath. "How much?" she asked, unable to find any logic in the question. "Ryan isn't for sale, Bryce. I brought him back because—"

Bryce slashed a hand through the air impatiently. "Let's cut the crap, honey. My son's been missing for almost five years, and you're expecting me to believe that he's turned up on my doorstep, fit as a fiddle?"

He shook his head, vexed at being taken for a fool. He'd been warned to expect this kind of thing—a crackpot showing up with his lost child in tow. Bryce had thought that was over with several years ago. He shook his head angrily. It just goes to prove that some people would try anything.

Yet Marlie Stynhearst knew something about Gordon. Or the boy did. The rhyme he recited had been known only by Gordon, it being written for him by his mother. Wary excitement scraped over Bryce's nerves like a currycomb. Could his son be alive? Could he trust this woman or the boy to tell him the truth? That he may not be able to disappointed him as much as angered him. There had been such wondrous promise in meeting Marlie. Now that promise could be a vicious trap awaiting him.

Unwilling to show his mixed feelings, he asked her nonchalantly, "What do you want with the reward money? Did you and your Rex discover that three's a crowd."

Marlie shook with anger until she felt her bones clank together. The monster. The unfeeling, idiotic monster. She'd been through hell and back to get Ryan safely home. Now he thought she wanted money for Ryan's return? With more nerve than she thought she possessed she walked over to Bryce. Facing him squarely, arms akimbo, she set him straight on the financial end of this matter.

"What would I want with your money? Your dear little AirShip facilities could cover the town of Sunnydale from one city limit to the other, plus employ every man and woman in residence, and it *still* wouldn't fill a hip pocket of Stynhearst Industries." She tapped her chest. "And I am Stynhearst Industries."

Bryce studied her a moment, judging her words, judging her. Finally he shrugged, an eyebrow hiked. "Time will tell, won't it? For now, I'll give your noble intentions the benefit of the doubt. So why did you bring my long-lost child home to me? Did it just come to you one day that maybe you should return the child to his father?"

"If you'll stop being a sarcastic, bullheaded brute, I'll be happy to tell you the whole story," she snapped.

Bryce grabbed her arm in an ungentle vice, pulled her over to the staircase and pushed her down on the bottom step. Bracing a foot beside her hip, he crossed his forearms over his knee and leaned close to her face. "I'll be as sarcastic and bullheaded as I please until I get answers to my questions. My son was kidnapped. That child with you knows something about him. So, talk. Tell me your entire, fascinating story."

Marlie licked her dry lips. Reminiscences of another time and place when she was trapped and cowed by a man curled viciously through her mind. She would become a victim again if she allowed it.

She lifted her chin and straightened her spine. She'd done nothing wrong; she wasn't the villain. "You heard Ryan recite the poem. If it were taught to your son by his mother, who else could Ryan be?''

"Any child can learn a poem," he said impatiently. "My first thought was that your kid had heard it from mine."

Marlie nodded. "Farfetched, but possible," she agreed. "If you'll hand me my purse from beside the front door, I'll show you more proof."

He complied, tossing her shoulder bag into her lap. From the zippered compartment, she pulled a small, leather-bound photo album. It contained a visual chronicle of Ryan's years, photos of a toddler, which Marlie had salvaged from her brother's personal effects, and photos she had added over the years.

She handed the album to Bryce. "Your proof," she said simply.

If someone had asked Bryce how he felt at this moment, he doubted seriously that he could have given a sensible answer. Too much nebulous hope was tied up in the moment, and he had experienced it all before—the high of daring to believe that a lead would give him back his son, only to discover that it was nothing more than a puff of smoke in a stiff breeze.

Admittedly, Bryce had never felt this close to the truth. It was a living presence in the room, beckoning him to believe one more time. With hands that would not stop trembling, he opened the book.

The first photograph was of a grinning child who Bryce had last seen nearly five years ago. Gordon. Bryce had spent happy hours enticing that same dimpled smile from those chubby cheeks, and the impish blue eyes could belong to no other.

The next photo depicted the same child, though his features had aged slightly. Bryce turned away from Marlie and braced his back against the newel post. Marlie's gentle hand upon his shoulder and her words, "I'll wait outside," barely registered. The world could have come to an end and still nothing would have distracted Bryce as he looked at picture after picture that charted the natural progression of months and years of a little boy whom Bryce remembered best as a baby swinging joyfully on the patio.

By the time Bryce closed the little album, his cheeks were wet. He breathed deeply, evenly, forcing himself to think one thought at a time, to feel one sensation at a time. It wasn't easy; too much wanted to come at him too quickly. Gordon was alive. Gordon was home. He was waiting outside, waiting with the woman who had known his son for more years than he had. Bryce wanted to rage and rejoice at the same time, for so much had been lost, yet so much waited to be reclaimed.

He wiped a hand across his face and slid the album into his hip pocket. The most uncertain steps he had ever taken in his life consisted of walking out the front door and facing a woman and a child. What did he say to his son who he hadn't seen, hadn't touched, in four and a half years? And what did he say to the woman who'd had the pleasure he'd been denied?

Looking at the two standing together on his porch, Bryce saw nothing but a solid force of resistance against him. The child wore a wary expression that should never have been cast upon a father, and Marlie wore a similar expression of wariness, though she took greater care in trying to hide it.

Oh, but Marlie Stynhearst was wary. She knew things. She knew things that Bryce wanted, needed, to know. But until he severed the solid bond between his son and this woman, he couldn't get his answers.

"I want to show you something," he said to the little boy, and took him by the hand to lead him away from the woman who had already had him for too long.

"Bryce," she called, and he could detect several emotions in her voice—all worthy their presence.

"Stay there," he called back to her. "I'll be back in a few minutes."

Marlie watched from the porch as Bryce led Ryan into a thick grove of birch and oak behind the house. Wringing her hands, she worried about what Bryce would tell the child. Had she done the wrong thing in not telling Ryan that they were traveling to Connecticut to meet his father?

At the time, it hadn't seemed necessary to worry the little boy with a relationship that he understood in principle but not in application. Marlie had been sure that once she, Ryan and the Powells had come to know one another, and the secrets of the past could be revealed, then the future could resume its natural course. A family would be reunited, and Marlie would be welcomed to help connect the past with the present, to help ease Ryan into his new role of son. With a few ill-chosen words, Bryce could make havoc of the delicate situation, and the blame would be Marlie's for not preparing Ryan better.

Bryce returned within the promised few minutes, but he returned alone. "Where's Ryan?" she demanded, searching the wooded edge of the lot. Ryan needed protecting; she couldn't leave him vulnerable for one moment.

Bryce didn't break stride as he mounted the step, grabbed her arm and began hauling her around to the other side of the porch. She dug in her heels, grasped the nearby railing and screamed, "Where's Ryan?"

Her genuine distress moved Bryce enough that he stopped and looked at her. "He's down by the lake, happily playing in an old tree house. Don't worry. He's a lot safer than you are right now, lady."

"You don't understand," she pleaded, refusing to heed his command to follow him. "Ryan—"

Bryce whipped her around, and within barely restrained violence, shoved her against the wall of the house. "You are so right," he snarled in her face. "I don't understand. But I will, or else I'll haul you down to the police station and let you explain it to Officer Vaughn. What will it be, Ms. Stynhearst?"

Ms. Stynhearst? she repeated numbly to herself. Had they regressed to starchy formalities again. The hope within her began dissipating like a morning dew under the hot summer sun as she searched the face of this man whom she had truly wanted to like. He had become a stranger again, as fearful and perhaps more dangerous in his own way than Rex. Had she made no worthwhile impression upon Ryan's father? Was the significance of her being at this place, surrendering her world into his care meaningless to him?

Of course she knew how Bryce felt. She was feeling it too. It was a whiff of fear with each breath she drew, a second of time gone with each beat of her heart. To know that she was going to lose something precious to her could be no easier to accept than waking to find that a thief in the night had visited.

"Please," she whispered to him, "stop hurting me."

The pressure on her arms slackened immediately, and Marlie realized that Bryce thought he was causing her physical pain. How she wished that physical pain was all that needed tending. She rubbed her numb arms and in a voice rusty from contained tears, said, "I know you have questions. I want to answer them for you."

And so she began to talk. She told him everything she knew for certain, and some things that she could only guess. She told him briefly of her life in Europe, of her return to the States to accept her inheritance of the Stynhearst conglomerate, and of taking custody of her small nephew.

The difficult part was confessing her acquaintance with Rex Kane. It embarrassed and shamed her to admit she had been engaged to the man who had committed this horrendous crime against Bryce and Ryan. The same feelings applied to telling Bryce of Rex's threats and blackmail, and of her gullibility in being lead by his evilness.

When her story ended, she looked at Bryce for the first time since she'd begun talking. When he finally asked coldly, "Can you prove any of this?" Marlie thought she might go out of her mind. Scrubbing her hands over her face in agitation, she thought of the cassette tape she'd taken from Rex's safe. It would prove her story. Oh, how she'd personally wanted to bring about Rex's downfall.

Sighing, she knew that Bryce deserved to know that this criminal could be caught and brought to justice. She owed Bryce that much peace of mind, didn't she? "We need a cassette player," she said, pulling the tape from her purse.

Bryce took the tape and motioned her to the Saab. He inserted it into the tape deck, then listened intently as the man, Rex Kane, talked away the next twenty or so years of his life. When the tape ended, Bryce sat still, savoring the first moments of absolute contentment he had experienced in a long time.

Eventually Marlie spoke, breaking the fragile web of peace. "Well?" she asked hesitantly.

Bryce inhaled deeply. Well, indeed. He looked at the beautiful woman beside him and felt regret mixed with hope. "If Nick Vaughn substantiates your story, we'll go from there." He didn't say that investigating would take time, nor what he would do about Marlie while they waited. He wouldn't allow worries about her to distract him now. He had to think of Gordon.

No, not Gordon, he corrected himself savagely. The baby Bryce had known was gone. He'd been replaced by a little stranger named Ryan. Obviously, Bryce was a stranger to the child, too. "Why didn't you tell my son about me?" he demanded angrily.

Marlie's fingers sank into the Saab's plush upholstery. "How, Bryce?" she cried. "How could I tell a six-year-old child about a father he can't remember? He has vague recollections of his adoptive father, but of you, as far as I know, none. I've been Ryan's parental authority for half his life. How could I tell him that I was going to dump him in the lap of a man he didn't know? A man I didn't even know."

Tears drizzled down her cheeks unnoticed as she pleaded with Bryce to understand something that she, herself, could only perceive with her heart. "He's always trusted me to do what was best for him, to take care of him. Abandoning him with a stranger would destroy that trust, and I was not willing to do that. I wanted time for all of us to know one another, to establish a rapport before all the frightening secrets were revealed. Do yourself a favor, Bryce. Don't rush Ryan into a relationship that he doesn't understand, and may, consequently, refuse to accept."

Marlie's unwanted wisdom rang warning bells inside Bryce's head. Hating it because he was denied the thrill of what should be a blessed reunion, he would still take her advice, for he had no wish to jeopardize the future. "Come with me to get my son," he said levelly. "I doubt he'll leave with me without you."

"Where are we going?" she asked.

Bryce didn't answer. Marlie followed, unable to offer herself one good reason for doing so. Bryce was communicating awful predictions in a body language that bode ill for anyone with the nerve to resist.

Crossing a rock fence, Marlie and Bryce waded through the green pasture dotted with bobbing Queen Anne's lace and black-eyed Susans. The short trip ended at a small lake edged with cattails and weeping willows swaying gracefully in the summer breeze. High in the boughs of a nearby elm perched a well-preserved tree house, and through its window beamed the face of a contented child. While Bryce called his son down to go meet a friend, Marlie looked around and saw a good place for a little boy to grow up.

For Marlie, the six-minute drive back to downtown Sunnydale passed with the pleasantness of a small animal caught in a steel trap. The sensation swelled to excruciating proportions when Bryce pulled the Saab into the parking lot of Sunnydale Police Station.

Bryce's friend, Nickolas Vaughn, was a policeman whose physical attributes rivaled Bryce's. After a brief introduction from Bryce and the obligatory offer of assistance from Officer Vaughn, Bryce got right down to the business of destroying Marlie's hope for peace in the foreseeable future.

Since this couldn't be happening to her, Marlie became two women—one standing before the desk of a man in uniform, the other standing back, and with wry humor, listening and watching the proceedings.

She was fingerprinted, then photographed, front and side views. That Bryce and Ryan participated, too, didn't fool her; this degradation was strictly for Marlie's benefit. She was suspect. And Bryce wasn't finished with her yet. He asked Officer Vaughn if he would show her and Ryan the inside of a jail cell. With a quizzical smile, the officer obliged, calling an old man from a back room to lead his "prisoners" to a cell.

Marlie finished wiping away the ink on her fingers with a damp towel provided, she supposed, for fastidious inmates. "May I have my purse now, please?" she requested. Then caustically she added, "I don't carry my hacksaw in it."

The brusque "no" she received from Bryce didn't surprise her. She took Ryan's hand and followed the old man, her head held high despite the cramp in her pride. The metal door of the cell slammed behind her with a finality that was frightening.

While Ryan gave an excited little leap onto the hard, narrow cot of the cell, enjoying this unparalleled entertainment, thoughts ran helter-skelter inside Marlie's head, all tagged with one overpowering theme: Everything was wrong. Impromptu events had derailed logical order, and she was being punished.

Bryce watched Nick Vaughn's eyes following Marlie's departure. He knew what Nick was seeing and felt jealousy explode in his chest like the unexpected detonation of a Molotov cocktail. The untimely, inappropriate sensation was ruthlessly heaved aside as he stepped into his friend's line of vision and stiff-armed his weight against the desk.

Nick's smile managed to convey both innocence and lust. "That sure was fun, Bryce. Mind telling me what we just did?"

Bryce pulled the small photo album from his pocket and handed it to Nick. Nick obligingly opened the cover to the first photograph. "This was your son, Gordon, wasn't it?" he asked quietly.

"Is. That is Gordon. Keep turning the pages."

Nick looked up sharply, then back to the album. He flipped forward, then backward, comparing. The last photo was of the little boy whose fingerprint profile rested on the green desk blotter. Nick didn't have to explain that he had managed to put two and two together to get four. He said, "If artistry is involved, the photographer was damn good." He tapped the photo album against his palm. "I can send these to the lab in D.C. and see what they can tell us."

Bryce straightened, took the album from Nick and returned it to his pocket. "I already know what they'll tell us. The little boy in your jail cell is my son."

Perceptively, Nick raised a skeptical eyebrow. "But...?"

"But he doesn't know it." Bryce sighed and shoved his hands into his pockets. There was nothing that Bryce felt he couldn't tell this man who had shared the worst times of his life. Nick had made up the entire Sunnydale constabulary at the time of Gordon's disappearance and had worked harder than three men to help locate the child. From his time with the NYPD, Nick was privy to an impressive network of information, and although it hadn't been enough to find Gordon, Bryce never doubted that the best help had been available. Why Nick Vaughn had taken his talents and skills from the big city and brought them to Sunnydale was a mystery, but no one in this small town was of a mind to complain.

Bryce played the tape of Rex Kane's confession, then concluded the tale with why Bryce's elation at being reunited with his son was curtailed by the little boy's attachment to Marlie Stynhearst.

Nick tugged on his bottom lip as he stared thoughtfully at Bryce for several moments. Finally he said, "You believe this woman could have had something to do with your son's actual kidnapping."

"That's what I was hoping you could tell me."

"I can prove or disprove she's Marlie Stynhearst in a few hours. Proving her guilt or innocent of a four-and-a-half-year-old kidnapping could take longer." He glanced down beside his desk. "In the meantime, a lady's handbag can tell many a secret."

"Be my guest."

Nick grinned. "Not hardly. I'd need a search warrant. You, on the other hand, are merely a citizen with a wayward nature." He plopped the purse on his desk. "So you can have the honors, and I'll be your witness that you swiped none of the contents."

"Thanks," Bryce said dryly. Feeling a bit as though he were peeking into a lady's lingerie drawer, he dumped the contents of Marlie's purse onto the desk blotter. He soon got over his feelings of invading her privacy when a plump roll of greenbacks followed the usual lipstick, compact and wallet. Bryce slipped the rubber band off the roll and rifled the crisp one-hundred-dollar bills. There was way more money in the wad than a woman could claim to need on even the most arduous shopping spree.

Nick cleared his throat. "Well, the lady doesn't seem to favor a wallet for conventional purposes. Maybe you should see what she does keep in there."

The lady kept several credit cards, a few bills of reasonable denominations and an ID card. The photo on the card was definitely Marlie—or Marlena, to be exact—Stynhearst of Los Angeles, California, date of birth placing her at age twenty-three.

"Could be fake," Nick said with reluctant practicality. "How about a driver's license?"

"No."

The leather swivel chair sighed against Nick's restless shifting position. "She drove Hap Hanson's truck...illegally it would seem. Anything else of interest in there?"

Bryce was about to say no when a photograph slipped from a slot in the wallet and fell to the desk. He picked it up and examined the man standing beside the woman claiming to be Marlena Stynhearst.

Bryce instantly put the man's face to the name he'd heard recently. "This is Rex Kane," he said, handing the photo to Nick. "About five years ago he approached me with a business proposition that didn't interest me. I thought at the time that with AirShip thriving, I didn't need to make any questionable East Coast transport deals. Kane didn't take my refusal too well."

"No, I guess not, since he decided to kidnap your son a few months later." Nick looked at Bryce steadily. "We're talking about an extremely unstable, potentially dangerous man, Bryce."

Bryce nodded, having already figured out that part. "Can you keep the woman for me a couple of hours while I talk to my son?"

"I can keep her a lot longer than that. Even if the purported Ms. Stynhearst is exactly who she says she is, she's still guilty of withholding evidence in a felony."

Bryce stared at the tape in Nick's hand as if it had suddenly grown horns and a tail. That tape would put his son's kidnapper away for years, but it could also put away Marlie Stynhearst. For more reasons than he cared to admit, he was reluctant to see that happen. He met Nick's eyes as he said softly, "I don't recall telling you where I came across that tape, Nick, and for the life of me, I can't seem to remember."

"Are you sure?"

He looked again at the tape, then back at Nick. "Until I understand what part this woman Stynhearst plays in my son's life, I need her closer at hand than the nearest federal penitentiary."

Nick nodded, but added, "Why don't you accidently forget Ms. Stynhearst's purse? Without her money and credit cards, she'll find her anchor dropped in Sunnydale. I can secure the perimeter of our fair city against other means of escape."

"Sounds sensible," Bryce agreed, inwardly shuddering at Nick's implacable methodicalness. If Marlie was guilty, Nick Vaughn was the man to bring her down hard. "How about springing my son from the slammer?"

Nick scooped the keys up from his desk. "Be careful, Bryce," he advised.

Ryan went with Mr. Powell, not because he wanted to but because Aunt Marlie said he had to. He promised to behave and not play any mean tricks on Mr. Powell, though Ryan had thought of some good ones, and thought Aunt Marlie a spoilsport for denying him.

Ryan and Mr. Powell went to the airfield of AirShip Freighting Company, and the man strapped Ryan into a plane he said was a Piper Cherokee 6. For fun, Mr. Powell placed a radio headset on Ryan's head and while waiting for runway clearance, explained about some of the buttons, knobs and levers used to guide the plane.

It was exciting, for Ryan had never been inside a cockpit during flight. Yet it was confusing because he *wanted* to be in the cockpit with Mr. Powell. For while Mr. Powell did look at Aunt Marlie in a gross, mushy way, he also played a tough game of Battling Baboons. Getting photographed, fingerprinted and sitting in a jail cell at the police station had been cool, too. All that was great, but the rest was awful.

Ryan would never admit it, but, on the inside where it didn't show, Mr. Powell scared him. Scared him more than nightmares, or being without Aunt Marlie or starting first grade without any friends.

Could a person like someone and not like them at the same time? Ryan wondered. He didn't know, but he sure did hate being all mixed up. And it was all Mr. Powell's fault.

Bryce was thinking his own similar adult version of the eccentricities of the human nature. His heart pounded and his palms sweated upon the yoke. He'd taken off from runways hundreds of times in his life, but today was different. Today he carried precious cargo—his son.

How many times had Bryce dreamed, in vain he had thought, of his son being exactly where he was at this moment? Yet, visions of Marlie Stynhearst's fear-ravaged face as she waved goodbye to them from that jail cell chipped away at his contentment. It wasn't right or fair that she intrude upon this moment. Nevertheless, she may as well be sitting beside him, counseling him on the best way to handle this delicate and new situation in which he found himself.

Giving up on ridding his mind of Marlie's haunting presence, he conceded to trying things her way first. His son was home, but many things could affect how he adjusted. With his heart in his throat, Bryce began lightly feeling his way toward that coveted linking of their past, present and future.

"I'm glad you decided to come flying with me," he told the little boy beside him via the headset radio.

"Me, too," Ryan agreed warily, yet truthfully. "I wish Aunt Marlie could have come, too, though."

Bryce's hands flexed upon yoke. "There's only two seats in this plane, son. We'd have had to haul her around in the back like cargo."

Ryan giggled. "She wouldn't have liked that."

Bryce grinned back wryly. "No. Probably not. Besides, we men have to have time to do special things by ourselves once in a while, don't you think?"

The child straightened a bit in his seat and grinned. "Yeah. Do you take lots of men riding in your plane?"

"Not many your age," he said, swallowing hard. "But if I had a son, I'd take him flying with me all the time."

Curiously, Ryan asked, "Why don't you get a son, then?"

Bryce glued his eyes to the windshield of his plane, knowing if he looked at the child beside him, he'd lose it. "I had a son once. A bad man stole him away from me a few years ago."

"Did you love your son a lot?"

"Yes. A lot."

"You could get another son, you know," Ryan said sagaciously. "There's lots of kids who need dads."

Easy, Powell, he warned himself. His heart beat a cadence that threatened to crack his ribs. "What about you? You don't have a dad."

Ryan appeared truly surprised by the question. "I don't need a dad. I have Aunt Marlie."

"There's lots of things your Aunt Marlie can't do that a dad can."

Pursing his lips, Ryan thought this out for several moments. Finally he said, "Maybe. But there's lots of things Aunt Marlie can do that a dad can't, and I love her most in the whole world. So I'm satisfied."

Bryce wanted to raise his fists and bellow in rage at this unfairness. Of course he wouldn't. He'd continue to reason with a six-year-old child who didn't know or care what he was giving away. "Suppose you found a man who wanted to be your dad very much, and who would love you the most in the whole world?"

Ryan grew cautious again. "Who?"

"Me."

For Bryce, the silence in the cockpit was a rubber band being slowly stretched to its limit. Ryan looked at him, genetic replicas of his own blue eyes reaching out to him with sweet, innocent compassion.

"I'm sorry about your little boy getting stolen," Ryan said. "Maybe if I didn't have Aunt Marlie, I could be your son. But Aunt Marlie needs me, Mr. Powell." Sensing that he'd distressed the man, Ryan hurried to add, "But I know how you could still be a dad. Last year in my kindergarten class, there was a boy who wasn't treated very well by his foster parents. I bet he would like to be your son."

Bryce Powell looked at the small boy beside him and manfully presented him with the proverbial stiff upper lip. Where it came from, Bryce had no idea. He had wept bitterly for his lost baby. At the graveside of his wife, his tears had flowed unashamedly. Today's defeat was no less wretched, yet for the sake of this child, he would save his pain for later.

Later, many things would happen. One of them would be calling Marlie Stynhearst to a reckoning. Whether she'd had anything to do with his son's actual kidnapping was almost irrelevant now, for she had taken his child away from him in a far more irrevocable way.

"You lied, Marlie Stynhearst," he whispered darkly. "You did steal my son."

Five

———

To say Bryce returned to the police station in a damaging frame of mind was like saying that a mad bull turned loose in the small barn could have serious ramifications. He and Ryan retrieved his Aunt Marlie, then Bryce went about his mission with an iron control reminiscent of his earlier years.

They returned to his house in the country, and Bryce sent Marlie inside and shooed Ryan back to the tree house. Knowing how those green eyes of Marlie's could chip away at his resolve, Bryce refused to look at her when he joined her in the living room. With easy mental acrobatics, he could imagine her as only what he wanted her to be—a pretty woman to woo into his arms. But she wasn't. She was deeply enmeshed in the worst nightmare of his life, and he wouldn't allow himself to forget that soon.

He began to pace, trying to put some order to his chaotic thoughts. He wanted to put his hands around Marlie's throat and squeeze the life out her for what he'd been through. Yet, if even one fourth of what she'd told him was the truth, then he couldn't blame her for what had happened years ago. Finally he looked at her patiently watching him from where she sat on the bottom step of the staircase. As he expected, nothing but blasted innocence staring back at him.

"How did your time with Ryan go?" she asked gently.

"I wasn't too encouraged," he responded, keeping his distance by leaning against the stone fireplace across the room.

"He didn't try to bomb your car, did he?" she inquired facetiously, hoping humor would break the unbearable tension.

"No. But he probably would have if you'd suggested it."

"I wouldn't have done that, Bryce," she insisted mildly, wrapping her fidgeting hands around her knees to still them.

Bryce lunged away from the fireplace to stride across the room. Stopping near her, he grasped the newel post in lieu of her more tender body parts. "Wouldn't you?" he ground out. "Why not? You've not spared me much so far."

Marlie's gaze wondered away from Bryce's angry face and focused on the stained-glass transom above the front door. "I never had any desire to hurt you, Bryce. If I had, I wouldn't have given you back your son."

"No!" he bellowed, slashing a hand through the air to emphasize the denial. "You're giving me back a child, yes, but you still have my son, Marlie. You have his love, his loyalty and his respect. How do I get that back?"

Marlie's disadvantage, of course, was that she hadn't thought to examine herself in a criminal light. "I don't understand your attitude, Bryce," she said honestly. "I didn't steal Ryan from you. I simply loved a little boy who needed me, and took for myself what he was willing to give. Why are you blaming me for something that wasn't my fault?"

"You mean, assuming I believe that you had nothing to do with my son's kidnapping?" he retorted, and ignored her sigh of annoyance. "Your question then becomes a matter of objective reasoning, Marlie. Intellectually, I know you'd be right. I couldn't blame you. But I'm not thinking objectively right now. I'm thinking as a father who's been denied his son for almost five years, and who's looking at a woman who's had the pleasure that should have been his."

Turning away from her, he shoved his hands through his hair angrily. "Every time I think of you holding my child on your lap while I was tormenting myself with his fate, I could shake the daylights out of you. For years I've had to wonder if he was alive or dead. Hungry. Abused. I felt every pain I imagined him feeling. I felt the terror and confusion that he must have felt. I bled my life away in tears while you sat in your supposed comfy mansion rocking my child to sleep each night."

When Marlie stood to cling to the banister, her movement caught his attention. He strode over to her and grasped her arms. "You want to know what it's been like for me?" he demanded, giving her small, jerky shakes to emphasize his inner torment. "I could show you. I could throw you out of here and keep you away from Ryan for the next five years. Of course you'd still have advantages that I didn't have. You'd know that Ryan was alive and well treated. You'd at least have the hope of seeing him again."

Marlie was crying, not because of Bryce's rough handling, but because the painful picture he had just painted would eventually become her reality. Couldn't he see this? She swallowed her sobs and searched his furious face. "I admit that unfortunately your choices in what happens now are few, but not nonexistent. You do have the choice of looking for the blessing of the past. Your son wasn't abused or left hungry. He lived to come back to you. You—"

"And I'm supposed to thank you for your tender mercies in caring for my son," Bryce cut in brusquely. "I was innocent, lady, yet sentenced to five years in a hellish prison of doubts and fears. Then you come along with your Pollyanna good cheer and expect me to thank you, the warden, for setting me free."

Marlie felt her patience slipping. What did he want from her? "You can't have it two ways, Bryce," she asserted. "Either you find comfort in knowing that all those fears for your son were groundless, or you wish that he was dead, to justify keeping the heartaches of the past alive." She shrugged. "There's nothing else I can do but reassure you."

It was the wrong thing to say. Marlie knew it the moment the impulsive words rushed from her mouth. Bryce's eyes flared with an unholy fire that demanded the sacrifice of her very soul for penitence. She shivered slightly as a lazy smile drifted across his face. His voice dripped over her like warm, sweet honey straight out of hell's kitchen.

"Oh, I'm sure I can think of something else you can do, Ms. Stynhearst."

"What?" she asked apprehensively.

"I'll let you know."

"And in the meantime?"

"We wait, Ms. Stynhearst."

Bryce took it into his head to do his waiting on the sofa in Marlie's apartment and nothing short of gunpoint would dissuade him from the notion. Marlie didn't own a gun, which under the circumstances was probably a good thing, so she put a confused and wary Ryan to bed and went to bed herself, leaving the man sitting in her living room. She was so exasperated with him that she didn't offer him even the most modest comforts of her home.

The deliberate oversight bothered her, and as she drifted off to sleep, she acknowledged the reason: Bryce Powell sleeping on her sofa offered her a feeling of safety that she hadn't experienced since fleeing from Rex. That alone deserved a pillow and blanket.

Marlie dressed the following morning in bright yellow shorts and a polka-dot top, their cheerful color meant to bolster her optimism. She hadn't left the entire job to her wardrobe choice, however. While she had showered, she'd devised a plan that could solve many problems. She found Bryce sitting at her kitchen table, his hands wrapped around a steaming mug of coffee. He'd apparently gone back to his apartment to shower and to change his sleep-rumpled clothing for neatly pressed khaki pants and navy polo shirt. She hoped his fresh appearance was indicative of his disposition, for now was the perfect opportunity to discuss her ideas.

She smiled a good morning and reached for another mug. "I've been thinking, Bryce. Now that you know Ryan is your son, I should go back to L.A. and take care of Rex Kane. The man belongs behind bars for what he's done, and the sooner he's there, the sooner we can all rest easier. While

I'm there, I thought I would have my program expansion team start putting together a report on the feasibility of opening a branch of Stynhearst Industries here in Sunnydale and contracting the transport of our products to AirShip. Not only would I be nearby if you and Ryan need me, but I could help insure Ryan's future by investing in your company.''

''Hush, Marlie.''

Marlie hushed. The deceptive calmness of the order implied that it was a good idea. She waited, and finally he deigned to explain why he was refusing her offer.

''First of all, you're not to get anywhere near Rex Kane. He's being taken care of, and all you have to do is what you're told. Don't ask again to go back to L.A. Second, I don't want your money or your investments. All I want is my son back, completely mine and happy about the situation. I spent a sleepless night on your short, lumpy couch, deciding the best way you can help me accomplish that.''

''I'm all ears, Mr. Powell,'' she said frostily, squeezing her coffee mug to keep her hands from shaking.

Bryce got up from the table. To burn nervous energy, he began opening cabinet doors as he continued talking, pretending to look for something for breakfast, and not really noticing there was nothing to be had. ''You see, Ms. Stynhearst, it has occurred to me that if I boot you out of Sunnydale, you'd take the heart of my son with you. That could set back our relationship for years, and I've already lost too many of those with him. It appears that if I want my son back, his Aunt Marlie will have to be part of the deal.''

Somehow the relief she should have felt with Bryce's admission that he needed her wasn't there. ''I intended to stay until I knew Ryan would be all right with you.''

''Did you? That's very commendable.'' He rushed on, knowing if he stopped to dwell on what he was about to do he'd lose his nerve. ''Am I to understand that it's within your commendable nature to do anything to help me regain my son?''

''Of course.''

Bryce's smile satanically. ''Good. You're going to marry me.''

Some invisible imp tried to knock Marlie's legs from beneath her. She grabbed the countertop and hung on. "Your sense of humor leaves a lot to be desired, Mr. Powell," she gasped incredulously.

The smile that bothered Marlie vanished in a blink of the eye. Bryce stalked over to stand before her and smiled another smile that offered no improvement over its predecessor. "I left my sense of humor a few thousand feet above the ground about eighteen hours ago, dear. I've been dead serious ever since."

"But...but...I can't marry you," she wailed.

"Why? Are you already married to Rex Kane?"

"No!"

"Then you can marry me. And you will, in three days."

"You're crazy," she breathed. "You can't make me marry you."

Bryce pursed his lips and tipped his head in agreement. "True. I can't make you say 'I do,' but I can make you wish you had."

Marlie stared at him, her mouth agape. He sounded as if he were taking his insanity seriously. Marlie was tempted to go back to bed so she could wake up from this nightmare. "You haven't been listening, Bryce. I'm not going anywhere until I'm certain Ryan will be all right. I have an apartment, plenty of money and time on my hands. I'll be right here in Sunnydale for as long as it takes to see Ryan happy. Marriage isn't necessary."

"You haven't been listening either, Marlie. You see, dear," he explained with infuriating calmness, "by marrying you, I'm insuring your cooperation. Marriage will also reassure my son that, as his stepmother, you'll be staying around."

Marlie returned to the pragmatic chore of pouring the coffee, needing to salvage something normal in the moment. Yesterday she'd submitted to the indignity of being treated like a common criminal. She'd hated it, but she'd submitted because she understood Bryce's fears. Today she was almost thankful for yesterday's indignities. "For Pete's sake, Bryce," she said, laughing nervously as she tried to fill her mug without spilling the coffee, "yesterday you had me down at the police station being fingerprinted. How can you even suggest marriage, feeling about me the way you do?"

A long, heavy moment passed before Bryce answered, "It's because of the way I feel about you that I am serious about this marriage, dear. If my son could wave you a cheerful goodbye, it wouldn't be necessary. But he can't, so you'll stay until he can." He pinned her to the wall with a look that dared her to doubt him. "There's very few things I wouldn't be willing to do in order to get my son back."

He took the coffeepot from her listless hands and placed it on the counter. "I can tell from the shell-shocked look on your face that you think I'm being ridiculous. But ridiculous or not, you're just going to have to humor me."

Glancing down past her bright yellow shorts, he frowned at her long, tanned legs, then turned her around and gave her a little shove toward the door. "Go get ready."

There was more to get ready for? Marlie wondered hysterically. She hadn't been ready for this much. She dug in her heels, and over her shoulder asked, "What am I supposed to be getting ready for now? An air raid?"

Bryce almost smiled. "To sign marriage applications and get blood tests. Now, do you want to go upstairs and dress, or do you want me to carry you up there and dress you myself?" Seeing the unwilling compliance on Marlie's face, Bryce shook his head sadly. "That's a pity, Ms. Stynhearst. I never had the pleasure of dressing a woman."

"But you're quite proficient at moving a woman's clothes the other way, Mr. Powell?"

"I'll let you answer that question yourself in three days," he said wryly. "Unless you're wanting the schedule moved up, I'd suggest you move out. In the meantime, I'll have Mrs. Cobb pick up Ryan. He'll be safe there, and with Nick's kids to play with, he'll be happy with her until after the honeymoon."

"Officer Vaughn has children?" she asked, surprised.

Bryce nodded. "Six-year-old twins—a boy and a girl."

Her eyebrow raised. "Funny, but from the way he acted at the police station, I didn't get the idea he was even married."

"He's not. But his marital status needn't concern you."

"You're right. It's my own marital status that concerns me, Mr. Powell. I happen to like it the way it is." Before he could raise another debate, she marched out of the kitchen.

Bryce was mistaken about Marlie's obligation to humor him, for she had to do no such thing. Human compassion obligated her to grant patience to a man who had already suffered enough, but there had to be a sensible limit to what she owed him. Marriage was above and beyond all reasonable expectations. This had to occur to him once her identity was verified.

But looking at Bryce now and seeing nothing but raw determination compelled Marlie to grant him—for a while—the humor he seemed to be lacking.

Two hours later, Marlie was reconsidering her generosity. If Bryce had left his humor a few thousand feet in the air yesterday, today hers was hitting rock bottom in the wake of his madness. She signed marriage applications. She surrendered her left arm to the questionable mercies of Betty the Witchnurse at the local clinic. On the fifth painful jab, the woman finally hit Marlie's vein. Her only consolation to the ordeal was that Bryce looked slightly green around the gills and a little regretful that she'd suffered.

He brought her back to her apartment after Katy, the waitress at the only café in Sunnydale, served them a quick lunch. Marlie wanted nothing more than to escape Bryce for a few peaceful moments, but she failed to eject herself from the Saab quickly enough. He grabbed her sore arm, and she gasped before she could check her reaction.

Bryce winced and let her go. "I'm sorry," he said.

"For once we agree on something," she snapped caustically.

His lips tightened. "Don't try to leave town, Marlie," he warned her.

Marlie's chin came up. "You'll find me a woman of my word, Bryce. I said I was staying until Ryan was safe. Now that I see how unstable you are, I have to wonder just who is Ryan's greatest threat. You or Rex Kane." Bryce looked ready to explode, but she refused to relent. "I'll be here until I'm satisfied that Ryan's in good hands."

* * *

Marlie was held prisoner in Sunnydale for the next three days. Bryce was suspiciously absent from the scene, yet everywhere she went in the small town, the power of his influence followed her. She knew she was watched constantly; the Sunnydale citizens were as discreet about their spying as Godzilla hiding behind a lamppost.

She missed Ryan terribly.

Needing to get away from her loneliness and the oppressive feeling of being surrounded by the enemy, Marlie went to Happy Hanson, hoping to rent his truck for a drive in the country. Happy didn't look as happy as usual. He gently but firmly refused the request, saying he had orders not to give his truck to strangers. Unbelievably, Mrs. Cobb entertained the same attitude, refusing to allow her to see Ryan.

It was like being back at boarding school, but worse; Marlie felt more alone than she'd ever been in her life and it frightened her. The whole town had branded her an outcast, and hatred for what Bryce had done burned in her breast. He had turned them all against her, and now, even if she managed to work out some arrangement to stay in Sunnydale, to open a branch of Stynhearst here, there would be a wall built of mistrust existing between herself and the townspeople.

At the end of Marlie's third day in exile, she saw a smiling Nick Vaughn walking toward her. She took no pleasure from the friendly overture; he was a friend of Bryce Powell's, which in this town translated as no friend of hers. She turned around, ignoring the man's call to wait.

A moment later, he was beside her. "Mind if I walk you home, Ms. Stynhearst?" he asked politely, easily matching her quick pace.

"Yes," she answered with equal politeness. It made no impression. Officer Vaughn avoided a hint as if it might give him a rash. His tolerant chuckle scrubbed at her nerves.

"I've come bearing good news, Ms. Stynhearst. Good news that rightfully should be told to Bryce first, but since I happened to see you alone—"

"Alone?" she said feigning incredulity. "Am I alone? My head's been in such a whirl lately, I hadn't noticed."

Nick nodded, passing her a commiserating smile. "I am sorry. But until we found out something about you, we couldn't take the chance of you leaving town. I told Mr. McFarland at the bus station not to sell you any tickets. From there, the news traveled via the town grapevine that you were suspected of something, though the townspeople didn't know what." He looked at her keenly. "Sunnydale protects its own, Ms. Stynhearst."

"And very thoroughly, too, Officer Vaughn. I've lived in some of the meanest cities in the world, but the Sunnydale inhabitants make street people look like Spanky and Our Gang."

"I think we can safely say that's behind you now. I got the confirmation on your identity and credentials a couple of hours ago."

"Well, that's a relief. I've been wondering if I was who I thought I was." Her eyes cut across to him. "I am, aren't I?"

Nick laughed. "You are. And it's truly a pleasure to meet you Ms. Marlena Stynhearst of Los Angeles, California, owner of Stynhearst Industries."

The brisk walk became a stroll. Marlie wasn't one to hold a grudge when someone was at least trying to be reasonable. And Nick Vaughn was. "I could have saved you a lot of trouble if you'd believed me in the first place," she said softly.

"Call me Nick, please. And I did."

Marlie looked at him sharply. "You did?"

"Uh-huh. Before I came to Sunnydale, I was a police detective in one of those cities you mentioned," he said. "So many shifty-eyed characters come through the precincts every day that a cop gets so he can hear a lie before a suspect even opens his mouth." He looked at Marlie and smiled. "Your mouth never struck me as suspicious, Ms. Stynhearst, though I couldn't take a chance of guessing wrong."

Marlie smiled back and felt better than she had in days. She had the law on her side now, and soon the Sunnydale residents would follow. Of course that accounted for less than half the opposition, since Bryce, alone, made up the majority of her troubles.

Nick took the house keys from Marlie's hand, unlocked the door and ushered her into the foyer. "I just wanted to stop by and tell you that Bryce should be a little easier to get along with from now on."

"That would be nice, but what would thrill me more is for Bryce to call off his insane wedding plans," she said pointedly.

Nick looked sincerely puzzled. "What wedding plans?"

"The ones I've been humoring him with," she said sardonically.

Nick took his time before answering. "Most men take their brides-to-be for a blood test, Marlie, not to be fingerprinted."

Marlie nodded agreement. "He's done that, too," she said, pulling up the three-quarter sleeve of her jersey shirt to display a large, ugly bruise on the inside of her elbow. "I've received the full Bryce Powell treatment. Naturally, now that he'll know who I am, he'll call a halt to this craziness, right?"

Nick Vaughn looked so doubtful that Marlie wanted to cry. "I won't marry him, Nick," she grated, physically trembling as she thought of the possibility.

"Hey, Marlie, don't worry until you have a reason," Nick gently chided, sliding a comforting arm around her.

As inopportune times go, this one ranked near disastrous. Bryce came through Marlie's front door, found his best friend and his fiancée in a cozy clinch and saw red. "What are you doing?" he asked of either who had the nerve to answer him.

Nick did. He held on to Marlie and replied flippantly, "I'm stealing this beautiful woman from under your nose."

"Friendship has its limits, Nick," Bryce said coolly.

Nick cocked an eyebrow, and a slow, understanding smile dawned. "So it does," he responded, stepping away from Marlie.

Marlie looked from one man to the other, catching the gist of their exchange and not liking it. She pointed an admonishing finger at Nick's nose. "You tell Bryce your news